FATAL
FIELD TRIP

MARCIA DOVE

Acknowledgments

This book is dedicated to my sister, Linda Legeyt, and my friend and mentor, Mary O'Connell. These women overcame many obstacles in their lives and stepped out of their comfort zones to pursue their dreams. I will forever be grateful to these role models for instilling in me the self-confidence I would need to carry on after losing Linda and my beloved husband Bill to cancer last year. Writing this book and its sequels have provided me with an outlet for sharing my grief and the complex process of starting life over after the loss of a loved one.

Introduction

M y father was killed in a tragic automobile accident when I was only three— I barely remember him. According to Mom, Dad named me after his great-grandmother, Maggie. He saw her picture once in an old family album and claimed I looked just like her. With my moon-shaped face, cornflower blue eyes, curly auburn hair, and the obligatory freckles he called 'Irish angel kisses,' he insisted Maggie McManus was the perfect name for me! I have no idea where that family photo album ended up, but all my relatives are long-sense departed.

Mom also wistfully told me that the name Maggie McManus reminded my father of one of their favorite Janis Joplin tunes, "Me and Molly McGee." When I feel disconnected, I play that song and turn up the volume

I was raised in Ashley, Massachusetts, a small sidewalk community in the suburbs of Boston. After Dad died, Mom said she had no desire to move or remarry. My mother, an elementary school teacher for the town of Ashley, enrolled me in all sorts of after-school activities; ballroom dancing and violin lessons absorbed much of my free time. We lived a relatively

1

uneventful life in the same house, a modest two-bedroom, two-story colonial, from the day I was born till I graduated from high school.

Living in a small town does have its advantages; everyone knows who you are, I could walk to school, and the library was right around the corner from our house. I became an avid reader, fancying murder mysteries— riding my bike around the neighborhood with a "spyglass" in my back pocket, envisioning myself as a future Nancy Drew. Nothing ever happened in our quiet, ordinary small town. Little did I know I would have ample opportunity to investigate real murders in my adult life!

I made it through high school with outstanding academic grades! However, Mom's primary consideration for college selection was its distance to our home in Ashley. Her world was a tiny circle, and she meant to keep it that way. I spent almost every weekend back home in Ashley during my college years.

But change was inevitable. With a Master's Degree in International Hotel and Tourism Management in hand, I accepted a high-level sales position in an upscale hotel near Boston, Massachusetts. My career fast-tracked to a general manager's role for a hotel and conference center in the Boston suburbs. That high-level position left me with limited free time, and visits to Mom became sporadic.

Mom had a hard time adjusting to living alone. Without me to rely on for company, she slowly began to try her wings. Much to my delight, she became a frequent visitor at the hotel. Becoming absorbed into some of the social activities required of a general manager, there became a noticeable difference in her. The new Mom was outgoing, relaxed, and happy.

I managed that thriving hotel for five years and loved every minute of it. But life has a way of throwing curveballs when you least expect them, and after some deep soul searching, I decided to change my career path and relocate to Florida. The factors surrounding those life-altering changes are a painful story with which I am still learning how to cope.

Chapter One

After months of job searching, I finally settled on a hospitality instructor's position at Panhandle State University (PSU). The university's location in the picturesque community of River Town, Florida, clinched the deal. I am totally enamored with this small sidewalk community with its quaint shops, older churches, and grand old historic homes, so reminiscent of my hometown Ashley, Massachusetts.

I have spent many a nostalgic moment in The Black Olive. Comparable to the old country stores in New England, it is a combination Italian restaurant and gift shop with much of its merchandise consisting of memorabilia and toys dating back to the forties and fifties.

River Town, just like many small communities, revolves around the Chamber of Commerce, whose goal is to further the interests of small businesses. After relocating to River Town, I stopped by the Chamber of Commerce office to introduce myself and apply for membership. The Chamber's Executive Director, Diana Ferguson, happily signed me up.

I asked Diana to recommend a few businesses that might benefit from working with PSU's Hospitality students. She handed me a directory and mentioned The River Town Hotel and Conference Center.

Gossip is central to most small-town mentalities; the chamber director proved to be no exception.

I dislike gossip, especially having witnessed the damage done by gossipers in my hometown of Ashley, who, without remorse, thought nothing of impugning the reputations of other residents. But I could not get away without Diana sharing the River Town Hotel and Conference Center's unsavory history.

"Every town has its stories, and River Town has many," Diana confided. "The hotel had been on a downward spiral for many years. In its run-down condition, with a terrible reputation to boot, most River Town residents avoided the hotel, fearful of tarnishing their reputations by associating with the unsavory characters who frequented the dying establishment."

In a conspiratorial tone, Diana added, "The hotel, located so close to the county courthouse, had been a blight on the community. The other downtown businesses complained about their loss of revenue; some even went out of business. It was impossible to attract new companies or even new residents to the area with this massive eyesore in the center of *their* town.

"The hotel was sold about a year ago. The town fathers and downtown merchants had breathed a sigh of relief when the new owners immediately commenced spending huge sums of money remodeling the rundown hotel."

Diana continued her tale, gushing on and on about the new Hotel General Manager, Johnathan "Trip" Evans. "Trip is a professional with a sterling reputation. The chamber members are thrilled at how quickly he has transformed the hotel. The hotel is once again hosting important events."

Diana stopped to take a sip of water. I feared in preparation for continuing her story. I quickly reached for my purse and stood up, thanking her for her assistance, telling her to please call on me if she needed me to volunteer for any committees, and rapidly departed.

I was excited, though, after hearing Diana's buildup of Trip Evans and the hotel! The hotel might prove to be one of the better community partners for my classes, providing field trips, lots of hands-on experiences for the many hospitality subjects I would be teaching. Possibly even internships.

I called Trip that afternoon. After introducing myself, I told him about my visit to the Chamber of Commerce and my meeting with Diana Ferguson, saying, "Diana thought you might be able to help me out. I want to take my Convention and Meeting Planning students on a meaningful field trip this semester; your hotel sounds ideal."

"Welcome to River Town, Maggie. Nice of Diana to think of us. I would be delighted to take the students on a hotel tour. They can watch the banquet set up staff in action, and Arlene Dahl, Meeting and Event Planner, can lecture the students about the hotel's event planning process. "By the way," he laughingly announced, "Arlene has the 'gift of gab,'

6

I suggest you set a limit on how long you want her to talk." We agreed on a date and time, thanking him profusely, I hung up.

A lot has happened since that phone conversation. I have been on a highly stressful learning curve, attending training sessions and creating four courses for an August startup. The semester has been in session for several weeks, and I am finally comfortable with the way my classes are going.

I feel a little lonely today and am lying in bed, contemplating my relocation to River Town, Florida. I have made a few acquaintances but no actual friends. Instructors work alone, so there are limited opportunities for interaction with my counterparts. It is too late now to worry about whether my decision to change career paths and relocate to sunny Florida is going to be one of those regrettable decisions people sometimes make in the heat of the moment.

My mother would have had plenty to say about my lying in bed indulging in self-pity. She would have quoted some idiom to make the point that I have only been here a few months to give it a chance.

I vividly remember as a child crying over something that had not gone my way and my mother trying to console me—stroking my hair, whispering, "Crying over spilled milk isn't going to solve anything." Mom was always citing idioms like that during my teenage years, something I found highly annoying. Now, I would give anything to listen to her calming voice, touting pearls of wisdom.

Determined to change my mindset, I threw off the covers and climbed out of bed. Coffee was always first. I doubted

7

I could start a day without that first cup. I sat at the dining room table, thinking about the exciting day ahead of me. Today is the long-awaited field trip to the River Town Hotel and Conference Center. Trip and Arlene will be meeting me in the hotel lobby at 9 a.m., an hour before the students are due to arrive.

I was providing Arlene with the questions the students would be asking after her lecture. I know this might seem odd, even bordering on cheating in some way, but the truth is, I realized I had put Arlene on the spot by allowing the students to include questions about her personal life. I need to share their intrusive questions with Arlene beforehand!

Depending on unforeseen traffic conditions, the River Town Hotel and Conference Center is about a ten-minute drive from my house. I glanced at my watch. It was only 6:30 a.m., plenty of time for a thirty-minute power walk around the neighborhood.

As soon as I moved to River Town, I began walking almost every day— heeding the words of a trusted counselor, "It may seem like a small thing, but just getting off the couch and putting one foot in front of the other is crucial to getting your life back on track." I admit I was willing to try anything that might make me feel better and took this literally. Walking, for me, is mood-elevating, creating a sense of tranquility and well-being. Most days, I feel optimistic that living a healthy, happy, productive life is still possible.

The purchase of a Fitbit tracker that serves as a watch and calculates steps, distance walked, calories burned, and active minutes has helped me monitor my progress and, most importantly, serves to keep me motivated.

My house, located in one of the new subdivisions that recently sprang up in River Town, has a sidewalk that winds around the neighborhood, making it ideal for walking. Early morning is the best time for me to walk; before my hectic daily schedule starts.

When my feet hit the pavement, most people are still asleep, and I can gawk unabashedly at the neighbor's houses, gardens, and manicured lawns. Often able to admire the interior of a home through a window when someone has either forgotten or not bothered to close the blinds.

I reasoned that paying attention to details is necessary, both as a former hotel general manager and in my new role as an educator. I cringed at the thought that my gawking might be viewed differently by others, finding my rationale flawed in some way and that my gawking constitutes being a busy body!

Tuesdays and Fridays are trash days, and I often see people in their pajamas or bathrobes putting out the trash. No one ever seems embarrassed, and they wave or call out good morning to me as I pass by. I love stopping to talk to the early morning dog walkers. Making a fuss over the owner's dogs, asking their names, and patting them elicits smiles and pride in ownership, much like the parents of small children.

Finishing my first cup of coffee, I returned to the bedroom and pulled on a pair of green spandex gym shorts and a matching shirt. I sat on the bench at the foot of my bed and laced up my walking shoes. Before setting out, I grabbed a bottle of water from the refrigerator.

Stepping off the front porch, I spotted my next-door neighbor, Clarence, returning home with his dog Max, a not-so-spry but friendly cocker spaniel. Clarence and his wife Rita are active retirees in their seventies. They spend a great deal of time at the River Town Seniors Center, taking advantage of all the activities offered by the community. I waived to Clarence, wishing him a great day, and set off at a steady walking pace, moving aside for the few joggers who flew past me. A half-hour passed way too quickly.

Returning home, I popped a coffee pod in the Keurig and turned on the television. While my coffee brewed, I placed an English muffin in the toaster and retrieved a jar of sugar-free strawberry preserves and a single serving of Greek yogurt from the refrigerator. Adding sweetener and Half & Half to my coffee, I sat down at the dining room table to eat breakfast and listen to the local news.

The newscasters bantered back and forth as they pre-sented Monday morning updates; local weather followed by the locals' misdeeds—auto accidents, robberies, and the like. Sunny skies were the only positive thing reported today. I cleared the table putting the dishes in the dishwasher. Despite the disturbing local news, I still felt upbeat and headed for the bedroom to dress for the field trip.

My walk-in closet is filled with suits, dresses, slacks, shoes, and accessories I had acquired over the many years spent shopping and bargain hunting with my mother. I couldn't help thinking about Mom's advice to me as a teenager, "Make yourself look like the best version of you every day. Your appearance should create a lasting impression on the people you encounter." I had taken this advice to heart, taking pride in my efforts to create colorful, coordinated ensembles.

Over the years, my clothing choices and gregarious, outgoing personality, I will admit, often left people smiling, laughing, or shaking their heads. Without a doubt, I always left lasting impressions— hopefully, favorable ones.

During the final session with my counselor, she asked, "Are you using your appearance to protect your insides from scrutiny?" I cautiously admitted, "That is possible. I know I need to look at my motives for my obsessive approach to clothing selection. I think I am finally ready to do that."

Seeming quite pleased with my answer, she had carefully scrutinized my face for any signs to the contrary before, finally saying, "That is progress, Maggie."

However, old habits die hard, and I began searching through my closet, choosing a royal blue pantsuit I had worn on many business occasions, still a perfect fit for my size eight, five-foot-three frame. Edward, my former boyfriend, had remarked that the suit's color matched my blue eyes. Since Edward was not one for handing out compliments, I hadn't forgotten that.

I removed a white turtleneck jersey from a hanger and pulled a bold red, white, and blue plaid silk scarf from a large pile of colorful scarfs stacked on a shelf. Pearl earrings, a pearl cluster ring, both birthday gifts from mom years ago, and versatile Rockport ballet flats that offered comfort and style completed my ensemble.

I showered, dressed, dried my long, curly auburn hair, applied eyelash booster, and my favorite lipstick, Dior Rouge—a fiery red hue with coral undertones. Affixing my name tag to the lapel of my jacket, I took a final look in the mirror. Smiling back is the illusion of a self-confident woman, with a smattering of freckles across her nose and cheeks. Retrieving my briefcase from my home office, I exited through the garage, backed my car out of the driveway, and I was on my way.

Chapter Two

The River Town Hotel and Conference Center is located in the older downtown section of River Town. The town received its name because of its location along the Deep Black River.

Swinging my black Chevy Camaro LT convertible into the hotel parking lot, I was surprised to see there were quite a few cars in the lot already. I pulled into the closest vacant spot to the front entrance. Turning off the engine, I sat in my car for a few minutes, admiring the facade of the imposing two-story red brick River Town Hotel and Conference Center. The tall windows across the front of the building, glistening in the sunlight, were outlined with black shutters and accentuated with window boxes filled with red geraniums and ivy. Beautifully manicured flower beds containing a fall assortment of yellow, white, and purple chrysanthemums and pansies bordered by purple and white ornamental kale showcased a brick walkway leading up to two massive glass entrance doors etched with the hotel's logo.

I love hotels, large or small; it doesn't matter. There is something magical about the hospitality industry as a whole, but visiting hotels creates a sense of wonder and excitement for me. My love affair with hotels began working one summer as a chambermaid at a guesthouse on Cape Cod. I loved finding ways to elicit surprise and smiles from the hotel's guests and discovered I was a born people-pleaser. That summer job was the impetus for my decision to pursue a career in hotel management. I have yet to come to terms with my quick departure from my last general manager's position, all part of the healing process that still seems to elude me.

Shaking off those gloomy thoughts, I changed focus back to the field trip. I was eager to see the inside of this hotel, especially, I am embarrassed to say, after listening to Diana's gossip. Entering the hotel, I approached the front desk, giving the receptionist my card, telling her I had an appointment with Mr. Evans and Ms. Dahl. The receptionist smiled and gestured to a bank of chairs, saying, "Make yourself comfortable, Professor McManus; I will let them know you've arrived."

Glancing around the lobby, I was impressed with what I saw. The room had a quiet elegance about it. The walls painted a subtle antique white were an excellent backdrop for artwork that appeared to be pictures of the hotel and River Town from a bygone era. Lovely green leafy print drapes hung alongside the tall windows overlooking the gardens and walkway to the front of the hotel.

A comfortable-looking overstuffed sofa and matching chairs, upholstered in a green and ivory companion fabric to the curtains, were clustered in front of an imposing floor-to-ceiling red brick fireplace. A portrait of the hotel's first owner, James A. Johnson, hung over the massive, cherry wood fireplace mantle. I was surprised by Johnson's stern facial expression. On closer observation, he appeared to be scowling. Portraits of hospitality people should show them smiling. What was the artist thinking, or perhaps Mr. Johnson was just naturally glum and didn't know how to smile?

I took a seat on one of the sofas. I had only been seated for a few minutes when a tall, slender man with a shock of beautiful dark graying hair, dressed in an impeccable black suit and red tie, strolled into the lobby. The man looking across the room at me was carefully assessing my appearance as well, scrutinizing my coordinated red, white, and blue outfit as he sauntered across the lobby in my direction.

I stood to greet him. Treating me to a generous smile, he picked up my right hand, giving it a gentle shake, continuing to hold on, introduced himself as Trip Evans, Hotel General Manager, expressing his delight in finally meeting me. Looking into his warm hazel-brown eyes, I had no idea that the general manager would be such a charming showstopper. I now know why the Chamber's Executive Director, Diana Ferguson, had gone on and on about him. Thank goodness Arlene arrived just at that moment, providing a welcome opportunity to regain my composure.

Trip subtlety dropped my hand. Since this was the first time Arlene, Trip, and I had formerly met, I thought I should introduce myself. Beaming at Arlene and then Trip, I said, "I am Maggie McManus, Hospitality Instructor for PSU; I am delighted to meet you both in person. I appreciate your seeing me before the students arrive."

Turning to face Arlene, I added, "I thought it might be helpful for you to have the questions the students will be asking ahead of time, Arlene."

Trip teasingly interceded, saying, "Thanks, Maggie, it would be embarrassing if she didn't know the answers." I blushed and, looking over at him, smartly replied, "Some of these young people were 'creative' with their questions. I was trying to be helpful." Winking at me, Trip said, "Arlene, please take Maggie to Meeting Room D so you can review those creative questions. I have a phone call to make. It shouldn't take long. I will join you as soon as I'm through." I couldn't help noticing Arlene chuckling as she replied, "Will do," and invited me to follow her. I admit I was embarrassed by Trip's fun-making off-hand remark, which left me feeling foolish!

We made our way through the lobby, down a long, wide hallway— noting the large, gold letters, A, B, and C, on the walls to the right of the meeting room doors. The doors for A and C were wide open in anticipation of the day's attendees. Both rooms were set up "auditorium-style" with chairs positioned in straight rows and a podium at the front of the room— the appropriate setting for a short lecture or a larger group that would not be taking extensive notes.

The rooms looked freshly painted and newly carpeted, part of the recent renovation, no doubt. The door to Meeting

Room B was closed with a Meeting in Progress sign prominently displayed on the door.

Darn, I should have checked the reader board in the lobby to see where my students will be meeting. It would also be helpful to know what other functions are being held in the hotel today.

Meeting Room D turned out to be a magnificent board room with high ceilings, crown molding, and walls painted a relaxing pale green. Positioned under a glittering brass and glass chandelier in the center of the room was a mahogany table with elaborately carved legs. Arranged around it were six round-backed swivel chairs covered in floral print fabric in varying tones of greens, pinks, and pale blues. Traditional high back chairs covered in a coordinated dark green fabric resided at either end of the table.

I deposited my briefcase on the table in front of a side chair. Arlene led me to a linen-covered table containing an elegant silver coffee service, white gold-rimmed plates with matching coffee cups and saucers, silver spoons, and forks invitingly lined up next to a small tray of fresh pastries. A brightly colored seasonal flower arrangement adorned the buffet table. Impressive and flattering, all this fuss over me! As a former GM, I had always been the one to make a fuss over other people.

Arlene poured coffee for the two of us and told me to help myself to the pastries. I added cream and sweetener to my coffee, passing on the pastries. Arlene placed a cherry danish on a plate, saying apologetically, "I am addicted to sugar and just can't resist." With that confession made, she picked up her cup of black coffee and danish and took them back to the table, taking a seat in the chair opposite mine.

I took a sip of my coffee before opening my briefcase and retrieving a file folder that I handed to Arlene. Thanking me, Arlene added, "I hope Trip didn't offend you; I'm sure he appreciates your thoughtfulness; he is a very thoughtful person himself." Arlene removed the pages from the file and reviewed them while she ate her pastry and sipped coffee.

I sat quietly, thinking about my two back-to-back Monday afternoon classes. This field trip replaced my first class. We are three weeks into the fall semester, and I have come to realize I tend to over-prepare and my lectures can be a bit disciplined; I vowed to work on spontaneity and lighten things up.

I heard Arlene chuckle from time to time and knew she had come upon one of those creative questions. My favorite is, "How do people in meeting planning jobs who work long hours balance their careers with family life?" My initial reaction was, "You have to be in a position to meet someone and have time for dating to get married! Working so many hours a week leaves you with limited time to socialize." I couldn't wait to hear Arlene's response.

Glancing at my watch, it was now 9:45 a.m. The students would be arriving for their tour, and Trip hadn't shown up yet. From first-hand experience, I know that hotel managers can get caught up in situations unable to break loose; emergencies have a way of cropping up at a moment's notice.

Also, looking at her watch, Arlene suggested we make our way back to the lobby; hopefully, Trip might be there. Arlene placed the questions back in the file folder, handed them to me, and I returned the file to my briefcase.

We had just entered the hallway when we spotted Trip heading in our direction. At his side was a tall platinum blond dressed in a short black leather mini skirt and a tight-fitting red V-neck sweater accentuating her ample breasts. Her knee-high shiny red high-heel boots were the perfect choice for that fashion statement!

Arlene whispered, "That's Hannah Johnson, Director of Sales and Marketing ... my boss." I didn't want to blurt out how unprofessional she looked and bit my lip. My mother would have said she was a tart; by definition, "A tease or a flirt, a girl likely to get disapproving looks from old people." Trip and Hannah waited for us to join them, and we all headed for the lobby.

The students had already started to arrive, and the lobby was filling up rapidly. Greeting them, I began taking attendance, leaving no time for a proper introduction to Hannah.

I approached Arlene with the news that everyone was present. Above the din of animated conversations, Arlene loudly announced that the students should follow her to Meeting Room C. As soon as the students were seated, I made my way to the podium. Standing next to Trip and Arlene, I provided a short but glowing introduction of our hosts. I turned the platform over to Trip, and Arlene and I took seats in the front row.

Trip delivered a welcome message that included a bit of history about the hotel. Thank goodness, not the sordid, unsavory story Diana shared with me! I was happy he was keeping the field trip upbeat!

Trip wrapped up his talk by telling the students he was taking them on a tour of the hotel, adding, "For your safety and out of respect for the hotel's guests, you need to stay together. Please do not wander off into any areas of the hotel on your own."

Our tour took us down another wide corridor, similar to the one we just left—this corridor contained two meeting rooms. We entered the first room, which was considerably larger than the room we had just left. Trip told us the room was in the process of being set up for a luncheon, a perfect opportunity for the students to watch the banquet set up crew in action as they rolled round tables into the room, placing chairs around them. The wait staff simultaneously covered the tables with tablecloths, adding dishes, glasses, and silverware.

We entered the second meeting room preset with tables and chairs arranged in parallel rows facing the front of the room. Trip explained, "This setup is classroom-style, as the name implies; it is an arrangement that supports interaction between the speaker and the audience."

Adjacent to the meeting rooms was an enormous banquet hall. Trip referred to this room as the ballroom— an imposing space, wallpapered in a subtle blue and white pattern with carpeting the exact shade of blue in the wallpaper. The room's high ceilings boasted several crystal chandeliers— devoid of furniture; apparently, no significant function scheduled today.

I couldn't help myself; I took the liberty of walking into the ballroom to have a closer look. The room was spectacular, the type of room in which I had always dreamed I would hold my wedding reception. I walked to the center of the ballroom, closed my eyes, and my feet just couldn't resist; after years of all those ballroom dance lessons, they just automatically formed the perfect box pattern, and I took a few turns around the ballroom. Trip and the students had followed me into the room, and when I stopped dancing and opened my eyes, the students started clapping. Trip was staring at me, grinning from ear to ear, obviously enjoying me making a fool of myself once again today!

Next on tour was the hotel dining room. The wait staff was in the process of clearing a few remaining tables from breakfast and re-setting them for lunch.

Gleaming floor-to-ceiling windows overlooked beautifully manicured gardens surrounding an octagonal swimming pool. The dining room, wallpapered in a white embossed pattern, was a sea of dining tables covered in pale pink cloths. Adding to the room's formality, highly polished silverware, sparkling crystal water, and wine glasses were placed in their appropriate places on each table. Crisp white linen napkins artfully folded into a "stuffed water goblet fold" were placed inside the crystal water glasses. In the center of each table were salt and pepper shakers, a sugar/sweetener caddy, and a crystal vase with a single pink rose. Elegant floral dining chairs, upholstered with the same green, pink, and blue fabric as the boardroom's swivel chairs, were positioned at the tables. Judging from the looks on the student's faces, they were duly impressed with this exquisite room, and so was I.

Our next stop was the kitchen. Trip cautioned us to be careful, saying, "Restaurant kitchens are notorious for slippery floors." The kitchen staff was prepping meals for what Trip called a relatively quiet day—lunch in the restaurant, a midmorning coffee break, and a luncheon scheduled in one of the meeting/banquet rooms, presumably the one we just saw being set up. Before leaving the kitchen, Trip stopped to say, "Mondays are Executive Chef Louie's day off." Looking back at me, he continued, "I am sure Chef Louie will be glad to provide the students with an overview of kitchen operations at another time."

Trip led the students and me back to Meeting Room C. Offering a farewell to the students, and with a smile and a wave in my direction, Trip left the room. Arlene was standing at the podium, waiting for the students to be seated before beginning.

I neglected to mention, Arlene is a striking-looking young lady of Swedish descent. Unlike her boss, Hannah, Arlene is a natural blond and had the good sense to dress professionally in a stylish navy-blue suit with a blue and white pinstriped blouse and navy-blue pumps. She had even thought to wear her name tag.

Greeting the students with a smile and a warm welcome, Arlene spoke for over thirty minutes, providing an overview of the hotel's process to book a meeting or an event. She explained the importance of the forms they use to record the details surrounding any function held at the hotel. To ensure there are no mix-ups in dates or room assignments, only one person, in their hotel's case, the director of sales and marketing, can log information in the function book, the "hotel's Bible." Completing her lecture, Arlene asked the students if they had any questions. Students eagerly pulled out the lists they had been working on in class.

Her response to the family life question: "I am not married, but if I were married with children, I would want a husband who is willing to share responsibility for the care of the children and our home." Perfect response. I could tell the students were impressed with all of Arlene's well-prepared answers, our little secret. I was glad Arlene hadn't said anything negative to dissuade students from a career in hospitality.

After the question-and-answer session, the students and I returned to the lobby. I listened to them talking animatedly among themselves. One by one, they drifted out of the hotel. I glanced at my watch; it was almost noon when the last student finally departed.

I was ready to leave the hotel when I realized I had left my briefcase in the boardroom. I walked back down the hall, smiling to myself about what a successful field trip this had been, the first of many more to come. The door to the boardroom was closed, causing me to be concerned that there might be another meeting in progress, even though there was no sign on the door.

Once again, I chastised myself for not checking the reader board in the lobby. Since there was no sound coming from the room, I slowly pulled the door open just enough to get a peek inside—no one was sitting at the table, and my briefcase was just where I left it. With a sigh of relief, I entered the room.

Like other hospitality professionals, the dreaded *food danger zone* is always on my mind. I glanced at the buffet table to see if the banquet staff had removed the pastries and cream, leaving no chance for anyone to use the cream if left unrefrigerated too long. What I saw stopped me in my tracks. The silver coffee pot was lying on the floor—spilled coffee, leaving dark brown stains on the beautiful carpet. Hannah was lying on the floor, her body partially covered by the tablecloth. One of her shiny red high heel boots protruded from under the cloth. My immediate reaction was, "Why would someone yank the tablecloth from the table to cover her?" I hurried over to see if I could help her. Hannah wasn't breathing, and fresh blood was seeping from under the tablecloth onto the carpeting.

Covering my mouth, I stifled a scream! What to do? Should I call 911 or the GM? If I were the GM in this situation, I would hope someone would contact me first! Thank goodness I had Trip's number in my cell phone. Trip answered on the second ring. I had all I could do to utter shakily, "She is dead!"

"Who is dead, and where are you?"

"Hannah," I faltered, remembering to add, "the boardroom - Meeting Room D." Cautioning me to stay put, he reassuringly said, "I am on my way." I hope Trip won't think I had anything to do with Hanna's death just because I found her body!

Chapter Three

T rip's office must be close by. He showed up inside of a minute. After surveying the room and seeing Hannah lying on the floor, he looked a little rattled himself. Even though she sure looked dead to me, he walked over to Hannah, knelt, taking her pulse, proclaiming, "Hannah *is* dead." Trip looked over at me and asked, "Are you OK?" I nervously replied, "I'm OK, now that you're here."

Trip closed and locked the board room door with us inside. He dialed 911 from his cell phone and called the front desk manager with instructions to notify the hotel staff that Meeting Room D was out of order. As an aside, he added, "I am expecting the police; send them to Meeting Room D as soon as they arrive," making no mention of Hannah lying dead on the floor.

Directing his full attention to me, he asked, "How long have you been in the room?"

"Only a few minutes. I came in to retrieve my briefcase."

Trip motioned to a seat at the boardroom table, and I gladly sat down. Pulling out the chair next to me, he joined me at the table to await the police. An awkward silence enveloped. After several minutes passed, I was the one to speak first, "Do you have any idea who might have killed Hannah?"

Trip replied, "She was not well-liked by her staff or most of the other employees for that matter."

I couldn't help wondering why Hannah was still on the payroll but only asked, "So, it might have been someone with a grudge?"

Realizing what he had just divulged, Trip added, "As the new GM, I inherited Hannah along with a few other employees. I am still working my way through an assessment of who I will retain, who needs to be retrained or let go." Adding the clarification, "I have been counseling Hannah for three months; she was on my 'let go list.'"

Trip's revelation that Hannah was on an expendable list elevated him immensely in my eyes. Hannah might not have lasted three whole weeks, never mind months, if I were the GM.

Trip did a convenient subject change by asking me questions about my position with PSU. He seemed impressed with my recent career change. I was relieved that he didn't ask me how that decision had come about. I wasn't ready to share my story with anyone yet, especially someone I barely knew.

Our conversation came to an abrupt halt when we heard a loud knock on the door, accompanied by the words, "Police." Trip unlocked the door, slowly opening it, leaving just enough room for the two officers to enter. Once they were inside, Trip quickly closed the door. I knew he was concerned that a guest or an employee might be lurking in the hallway, curious about what was happening inside.

The officers, flashing their badges, introduced themselves as Detectives Callahan and Barker. Trip introduced himself as Trip Evans, Hotel General Manager, adding, "This is Maggie McManus, the person who found the body"—a segue into why Trip had called them.

Trip pointed to Hannah lying on the floor.

Detective Callahan lumbered across the room with Barker on his heels. Standing over Hannah's body, ironically saying nothing about her body being partially covered with a table cloth. A surreal moment, I thought, like something out of the TV crime shows I watch, *CSI* being my favorite, or reruns of the *Murder She Wrote* mystery series.

It didn't take long for Detectives Callahan and Barker to determine that Hannah was dead. This beautiful board room was now officially a crime scene. Detective Callahan called police headquarters requesting they send for the medical examiner.

I couldn't help but think that Hannah's death would soon be all over the local news—terrible publicity for the newly renovated River Town Hotel and Conference Center.

The board room would soon be cordoned off with yellow crime scene tape, leaving the GM to deal with the lost revenue and phones ringing off the hook. Undoubtedly, the hotel would be swarming with *looky-loos,* people who wanted to see what was going on for themselves. Trip would have his hands full. Hopefully, the detectives would find the killer soon, and things would get back to normal quickly.

From reading so many mystery books, I knew that I might not be going anywhere for a while. The detectives were sure to have questions for Trip and me. I told Trip and the officers I was feeling on edge and a little shaky and could sure use a cup of coffee. Trip looked questioningly at the detectives, offering to fetch coffee for them as well. Callahan replied, "Sure, we'd love some."

Detectives Callahan and Barker sat down at the table across from me to await the medical examiner. While waiting for Trip to return with the much-needed coffee, I had a chance to study the two detectives. At the moment, they were ignoring me, conversing between themselves and making notes about the crime scene. There was no missing Callahan's superiority attitude which was off-putting but leaving no doubt about who was in charge.

Callahan's rumpled ill-fitting dark brown suit and navy-blue shirt were attention-getting for all the wrong reasons. He was a short man with a healthy head of dark brown hair desperately needing a trim; whether he had shaved today was questionable. His disheveled appearance reminded me of the bumbling but clever Columbo character, minus the raincoat, from the TV series of the same name.

Callahan finally turned his attention to me. Attempting to intimidate me with his arrogant attitude and unsmiling misty gray eyes, he told me Detective Barker would be interviewing me, and he hoped I would cooperate with him.

Barker, a tall man, had noticeably towered over Callahan. Also drawing attention was his imposing figure impeccably dressed in a black suit with a pale blue shirt and a geometric print tie of varying blues, drawing you into his electric blue eyes, a dead giveaway for a big ego.

Barker's appearance may have been far more professional, but his smug attitude was equally offensive. Looking quite sure of himself, Detective Barker affixed those electric blue eyes on me as he took a notebook and pen out of a jacket pocket, ready to begin grilling me.

These condescending detectives gave me a good reason to be concerned that I might be considered a suspect since I was the one who found the body. I didn't have anything to tell them about Hannah. Our brief encounter in the hallway didn't constitute knowing her. That didn't stop Barker from asking me exactly who I was and how I had come to be the one to find the body? I told Barker I was a university professor and was here on a field trip with a group of students who had departed earlier.

"How well do you know the deceased?"

"Not at all. I saw Hannah in the hallway earlier today, but we were never formally introduced."

Barker's next question gave me pause, "What was your impression of her?" Then coaching; "Did she look frightened or concerned about something?"

I was not about to tell them that my first impression was she was dressed inappropriately for her position as director of sales and marketing and or that my mother would have labeled her a *tart*. I also wouldn't tell them that Hannah was on Trip's "expendable list" slated for termination!

"She looked OK to me." was the best I could do.

Thank goodness, Trip wasn't gone very long. I was becoming more and more uncomfortable sitting by myself with these two detectives glaring at me. The lasting impression I would make on them would have nothing to do with my carefully selected ensemble and a lot to do with whether I appeared to be a suspect in Hannah's murder.

Drinking coffee in a room with a corpse was a first for me; the coffee did manage to perk me up. After a few more questions about why I was at the hotel that day, Detective Barker dismissed me. I knew I was lucky to be leaving so soon.

I picked up my briefcase, happy that the detectives had decided it was not evidence. Before I could make my way to the door, Detective Callahan's parting admonishing words, "Don't leave town; we may have more questions," made me feel like a wayward child!

Really, where would I go? I have just bought a house and started my new job! I looked over at Trip, thanking him once again for hosting my students. I did not envy Trip. I suspected his day would become even more of a nightmare!

Making my way to the lobby, I exited the front door with a quick wave at the front desk receptionist. It was now two o'clock. Still feeling a bit unhinged, I was glad I had time to go home and try to unwind before my 5 p.m. class.

Chapter Four

T ry as I might, I could not get the picture of Hannah lying on the floor in the boardroom out of my mind. Disturbing as it was, I will admit, I was a bit curious about who might have killed her and how. I hadn't seen a weapon, of any kind, like a knife or a gun next to her. The part of her body not covered by the tablecloth showed no visible signs of a stabbing, gunshot wound, or blow to her body, leaving in question the area under the cloth not apparent to Trip and me. So, I mused, Hannah must have cried out. Someone might have heard her or seen something. Hopefully, the detectives will find witnesses when they begin their investigation.

It was time to leave for school—the PSU campus is about a twenty-minute drive from my home. I hoped working with my students would create a much-needed diversion. I had made a point of arriving early for my classes. Students had also started coming well before the course start time, taking advantage of the opportunity to talk to me about their future in the industry, current jobs, family, or just anything at all. Three of the students who had attended the field trip to the River

Town Hotel and Conference Center that morning, also taking my afternoon class, arrived early.

The classroom was soon abuzz with talk about the field trip. Of course, none of the students knew about Hannah's murder yet, and I was not about to divulge that. Once the news broke, I was sure my name would be all over the TV and in newspapers. I would have no choice when asked but to admit that, indeed, I was the one who had found Hannah's body. Students continued to wander in, and I started class promptly at 5 p.m. We had a lot to cover in this two-and-a-half-hour class. The focal point of this evening's class was the assignment of group projects.

Projects for the Services Marketing Course entailed students entering a hospitality facility with the intent of critiquing its employee's customer service skills. It would take a hefty dose of humility for any manager to sit quietly and listen to students expound on the low quality of service perceived by their customers!

I had contacted several local hospitality businesses listed in the chamber directory, and several of them, knowing this, still agreed to work with the students. The River Town Hotel and Conference Center was one of the businesses that had decided to participate. Trip had assured me that the Director of Sales and Marketing, Hannah Johnson, would be happy to work with students on a marketing project. Who knew that Hannah Johnson would be dead when I handed out the group assignments this evening! I must have been unnerved not to have thought about that before I left the hotel today. My short-sightedness could prove awkward. I would have to call Trip in the morning to ask if the students could still work with the hotel on their marketing project?

I remembered the stress of group projects from my college days. Undoubtedly, the same issues of who my group members would be and where they lived would also concern these students. In anticipation of the whining, I had already divided the twenty-five students into five groups based on where they lived. Personality issues were something I really could not address, but I knew they were bound to come up. I gave the students the names of their group members, instructing them to get together and elect a group leader. Adding, "Choose wisely because this is the person who will be coordinating your group project, which can have either a positive or negative effect on your group's grade." A mad shuffling of seats and belongings ensued.

To keep the process fair, I had written the names of all five participating businesses on separate pieces of paper. Except for the River Town Hotel and Conference Center, I had also included contact information. I placed the folded pieces of paper in a paper cup. The group leaders selected one of the names from the container. Per my instructions, they began working with their group members to formulate a plan for getting started.

I immediately singled out the River Town Hotel and Conference Center group and quietly revealed, "I need to speak to the hotel GM before anyone contacts the hotel." I was thankful Kimberly, the new group leader, never asked why. I promised to call her once I knew who their connection would be. I adjourned the class at 7:30 p.m. A successful class meeting, except for the uncertainty of whether students could still work with the River Town Hotel and Conference Center.

Exhausted and hungry, I realized that I had skipped lunch. With the stress of finding Hannah's dead body and meeting with the police detectives, comfort food was in order. The Village Inn was on my way home. They make the best grilled cheese sandwiches—American cheddar, Monterey Jack, and mozzarella cheese with hickory-smoked bacon and grilled tomato slices on parmesan-crusted bread. I paired the sandwich with a cup of tomato basil soup, followed by a healthy portion of peach pie, topped with whipped cream. I felt a lot better after consuming all that comfort food. I paid my bill, left a generous tip, and headed the Camaro toward home.

Chapter Five

I awoke at 6 a.m. with a heavy heart, remembering that Hannah was dead, and I needed to call Trip to discuss continuing the student's marketing project. It was too early to call him, so I decided to fit in a morning walk. Tuesday is trash day, so I wheeled my trash to the curb before setting out. A few other people were wheeling their trash cans out as I made my rounds. I didn't stop to talk to anyone this morning; I just waved as I passed by. Returning home, I fixed myself a cup of coffee and prepared a boiled egg, seven-grain toast with margarine, and a glass of V8 juice.

After breakfast, I felt a little perkier and headed for the bathroom to take a hot shower. Toweling off, I wrapped the towel around myself and wandered into my closet. I was pushing the black dresses aside, deeming them way too depressing, when I spotted a knee-length purple dress with a round neckline and three-quarter length sleeves trimmed in black satin fabric. The purple color made me smile, so I took it off the rack and slipped it on, fastening a black patent leather belt around my waist and adding diamond stud earrings and a tennis bracelet.

I sat down on the bench at the foot of my bed to slip on a pair of black patent leather pumps.

My purple dress had me thinking about my mother. A creature of habit, not only had Mom lived in the same house all her adult life, but she had devoted a lifetime working for the same school system. Her limited social life was structured around our church; she loved being at home working in her garden and reading; doing things she could enjoy by herself. Mom was reserved and not much of a joiner.

After Mom retired from teaching, our neighbor, Helen, also a retired teacher, talked Mom into joining the Red Hat Society, a women's social organization. Their meetings create an opportunity for like-minded women to connect—enriching lives through the power of friendship. One of the membership trademarks is wearing outlandish purple and red clothing accompanied by large hats.

I couldn't help reminiscing about visiting Mom when she attended her first Red Hat meeting. Sitting on the bed in her bedroom, I watched her get dressed in clothing totally out of character for her! She slipped on a form-fitting, long-sleeved purple dress and stepped into red high heels. After applying mascara and red lipstick, creating a stark contrast with her lovely snow-white hair, she placed her wide-brimmed red hat jauntily on her head. Mom's magical transformation was reticent of Frosty the Snow Mans when he placed an old top hat on his head and began to dance around! Mom's electric blue eyes, usually quite solemn, crinkled at the corners, and her red lips parted into a huge smile as she viewed her appearance in a full-length mirror! She had turned to me for final approval. I told her she looked stunning; prepare for people to gawk, and the tongue waging that would surely follow!

Mom had picked up her pocketbook, saying. "I don't know what time I will be back; Helen is driving." With her head held high, adjusting her gait to accommodate her high heels, she headed out the door for Helen's house. I remembered telling her not to hurry home on my account; I was in the middle of reading an exciting mystery!

My counselor had told me that at some point, I would be able to look back at memories of my mother and be able to smile. I was glad that I could finally reminisce about my mother through that lens!

Glancing at my watch, it was now 8:15 a.m. I wanted to talk to Trip before I had to leave for a 10 a.m. faculty meeting. Hoping he would already be at the hotel, I dialed his office. Once again, Trip answered on the second ring, leaving me to think that this must be one of the hotel's guest relations protocols.

I asked him how he was doing? To which he replied, "After yesterday's nightmare, so far, today is off to a much better start." He went on to tell me, "The medical examiner arrived right after you left. His examination took about an hour and a half. Thank goodness the ME authorized the removal of Hannah's body from the boardroom shortly thereafter. The police detectives spent all afternoon and evening interviewing people. I didn't get home until almost midnight."

Trip thoughtfully asked, "How is your day going?"

"OK, but I do have a concern I need to discuss with you." Reminding him about the Services Marketing Project, asking, "Trip, in light of Hannah's murder, do you feel comfortable continuing with the project?"

Trip was silent for a minute before he responded with his version of the classic 'the show must go on.' "From my point of view, life offers a variety of daily challenges. It serves no purpose to shelter students from these experiences, even death." I told Trip that this project, "An Application of Services Marketing Principles," might help the hotel recover from the long-standing adverse effects the hotel has undergone.

When Trip and I had initially discussed the project, he had reiterated what the chamber director had told me about the hotel's history. He expanded on the hotel's run-down condition, bad reputation, and the enormous amount of money the owners had invested to bring the hotel back to life. He also told me he had received questions from many previous guests about what had changed other than a "facelift" for the hotel and why they should give it another chance? Hannah's death would add to the negativity, creating an additional obstacle to overcome.

Based on the student's interviews with customers, I told Trip they could determine if Trip and his employees had successfully defused customer concerns about Hannah's death, the hotel's unsavory history, and poor service quality? If not, the students would recommend customer service strategies Trip could implement to improve guest satisfaction and squelch negativity. I was relieved that Trip had agreed to go forward with the project.

With Hannah out of the picture, I assumed we would be working with Arlene and said so. Trip's matter-of-fact response, "On the contrary, because of the sensitivity of the situation, I will work with the students myself."

What great luck; my students will be working directly with the hotel GM. I gratefully replied, "I appreciate your willingness to spend some of your precious time with us."

Trip changed the subject, telling me he had called an employee meeting later in the day. He wanted the employees to hear from him firsthand about Hannah's death. He planned to reinforce what they should be telling hotel guests about changes in ownership and management; even more importantly, what to say about Hannah's death. He reiterated, "Of primary concern, no one should respond to any questions from the media. As general manager, I am the only spokesperson for the hotel." The hotel did not need this additional negative press. I knew Trip would have to find a way to calm the waters.

My wheels were spinning, and I asked, "Would it make sense to have the students attend their first meeting with you this week? They, too, need to know what to say about Hannah's death. Disseminating information to everyone as quickly as possible would be helpful." Without hesitating, he replied, "That, Ms. McManus, is a terrific idea! I will email you with some tentative days and times. I suspect the media will be all over this today, and the sooner I prepare the staff and the students, the better." With that, he said, "Got to go, Maggie," and hung up.

Looking at my watch, I realized confirming the group project with Trip had taken more time than I thought it would. I had to leave in ten minutes to be on time for my department's meeting. This meeting was the kick-off meeting for the semester and would last all day. I dreaded telling my boss, Dr. Caruthers, about my field trip, culminating in finding Hannah's dead body and getting an interview with the local police.

I made the meeting with barely any time to spare. Hard as I tried all day, it was impossible to get Dr. Caruthers's attention. To make matters worse, oddly enough, she was called away before the meeting ended, telling us her assistant would be finishing up the session. I did not think it advisable to tell anyone else about Hannah's death. I decided I would call Dr. Caruthers first thing in the morning.

I returned home and changed into jeans and a short-sleeved shirt. Settling down on the couch, I turned on the local TV channel. The 6 p.m. news had already started; I quickly learned that "the cat was out of the bag" … the reporter covering the story of Hannah's death had interviewed Trip that afternoon. There were pictures of the board room, wrapped in yellow crime scene tape, minus the coffee pot, broken china, and other debris.

The ugly stains from coffee and blood were still visible on the rug. I wondered if it would be possible to remove the stains or if Trip would have to have that section of the carpet repaired? I sure hoped he had left-over carpet from the renovation. I digress, sorry, once a hotel GM always a hotel GM!

Sure enough, just as I suspected, my name was mentioned as the one who had found the body. My phone was sure to be ringing off the hook tomorrow between the media, faculty, perhaps students, and of course, news box curiosity seekers. Even though I had planned to call Dr. Caruthers first thing in the morning, no doubt once she heard the news, calling me would be on the top of her to-do list. Whether I had any control over it or not, the negative press was detrimental to the university's reputation.

I spent another restless night tossing and turning, picturing Hannah's body in the boardroom, mulling over various scenarios in my mind about how she might have been killed and by whom. My phone rang at 7 a.m., and, no surprise, it was Dr. Caruthers. She sounded pretty calm when she put forth, "I watched the 6 p.m. news last night. Please tell me what happened?"

I apologized, saying, "I am sorry you had to hear the bad news on TV. I planned to tell you after the meeting, but I knew you must have had something important to contend with when you unexpectedly left early. I decided my news could wait till morning. I was planning on calling your office at 9:00 a.m."

I gave her my account of what had happened. Although she seemed sympathetic, her primary reason for calling was to warn me not to talk to the media. She would have someone from PSU Media Relations contact me.

"How should I approach the subject with my students?"

"Maggie, before you say anything to the students, ask that question of the PSU Media Relations Representative. Maintaining continuity in the information disseminated is important."

I hung up after affirming, "I understood and couldn't agree more."

Chapter Six

G osh, what a week, and it was only Wednesday. Once the River Town Rotary Club Membership Committee received a glowing recommendation from the president of my former Massachusetts club, they had happily accepted me as a new member. The club meets every Wednesday at noon at none other than the River Town Hotel and Conference Center.

I will be attending my first meeting today. Based on diversity, Rotary Club membership means they do not want too many members from any one industry. I believe I am the only PSU employee who is a member of the River Town Club; thus, I would be representing my university. Having had an excellent relationship with the Massachusetts club members, I am looking forward to interacting with the River Town members.

I arrived fifteen minutes early to "network," signed in, paid for my lunch, and wandered into the meeting room; ironically, it was the same dining space that was in the process of being set for a luncheon on Monday. Had somebody scheduled the meeting in this room because it was the farthest from the crime scene? No, of course not! My imagination is working overtime again; it is the largest meeting space other than the ballroom!

Looking around, there were about fifteen other early birds already in the throes of networking.

I recognized Mark, the owner of the River Front Restaurant, from his TV ad. He and a local insurance agent I met when seeking quotes on my house insurance whose name I could not remember were involved in an intense conversation. I did not want to interrupt them and scanned the room further for anyone else seeking to network.

I felt a tap on my shoulder and turned around. Greeting me was a tall, slender, stylishly dressed, striking brunette who smiled down at me and began, "You must be new. I don't believe I have seen you here before. I am Sara Milligan, the owner of Dress for Success."

"Nice to meet you, Sara. Yes, this is my first River Town Rotary Club meeting; Maggie McManus, Hospitality Instructor for PSU. I have passed your women's apparel shop many times. I am looking forward to finding time to visit your shop." Being the clotheshorse I am, this was no lie.

We chatted for a few minutes exchanging the usual get-acquainted information—where we lived, marital status, and interests—seeking areas of commonality in our lives. Sara asked for my cell phone number, gave me hers, and we updated our phone contact information. I was pleased that she wanted to pursue a friendship with me.

Sara then walked me around the room, introducing me to some of the other members. A few minutes before the meeting started, we sat down at a table for six—reticent of "musical chairs," three other people sat down rather quickly at our table. The remaining seat next to me, much to my delight, was taken by none other than Trip Evans. I had no idea he was a Rotary Club member. Trip told me he had spotted me when he came in and needed to talk to me after the meeting.

Sara, almost too quickly, interjected, "You two know each other?"

I smiled at Trip before looking back at Sara and explaining, "We finally met for the first time in person on Monday. Trip was kind enough to host a field trip for a group of hospitality students."

The president called the meeting to order, leaving Sara no time to comment. We recited the Pledge of Allegiance, the minister from the Methodist Church gave the blessing, and the wait staff began serving lunch. Curiously, during lunch, no one at our table asked Trip about Monday's 6 p.m. news.

Lunch was not the traditional banquet chicken, green beans, and baked potato that many restaurants serve for group gatherings. Instead, our superb meal consisted of a lunch portion of *Cajun Pasta:* Tender chunks of Cajun-seasoned chicken and shrimp served over fettuccine noodles tossed in a spicy cream sauce. Dessert was a slice of a "to die for" *Orange Sunshine Cake:* Triple-layer orange cake with a thin layer of icing in the middle of each layer. The top layer was smothered with whipped orange frosting and artfully garnished with a few tiny tangerine slices. I will need to add more time to my morning power walks if I continue eating like this!

The room was relatively quiet during lunch. People were busy enjoying their meal. The president resumed the meeting while the wait staff cleared the tables. The first item on the meeting agenda was new members and visiting Rotarians. As it turned out, I was the only new member this week. After the president's warm-hearted introduction of me and the visiting Rotarian from Alabama, he moved on to committee reports and fundraising.

The Rotary Club's motto is "Service Above Self." Members are always looking for worthwhile causes to support, which, of course, require money for funding. Just before the meeting adjourned, Trip caught my eye, mouthing, "Can you stay for a few minutes after the meeting?"

Smiling, I nodded my assent.

The room emptied quickly; although a few people glanced over at Trip on their way out, no one approached him. I watched people slapping others on the back, shaking hands, hurrying out the door to return to work.

Sara rising from her seat, hesitated at the table a moment; I told her it was nice to meet her, and I hoped our paths crossed again soon. Sara mumbled something like, "Likewise." I finally realized that Sara was waiting for Trip to acknowledge her; he didn't, so she left.

Once Trip and I were sitting at the table alone, he told me that he had sent me an email with potential dates and times to meet with my students. "I am hoping that this Friday might work."

"Students might balk at attending a meeting on a Friday; they often work on weekends. Given the importance of the issue, Trip, I will push for Friday, midmorning."

I was surprised when Trip just thanked me; not responding in his usual upbeat manner caused me to study his face. Trip looked tired, and I empathetically offered, "I am sure yesterday was another long day."

"Yes, a challenging one, to be sure. Media outlets were at the hotel a good part of the afternoon, asking questions and taking pictures."

"I watched the 6 p.m. news and thought you handled the interview admirably."

"Thank you, Maggie; I appreciate that and kind of you to say. By the way, the meeting with the employees went well. I am looking forward to an equally successful meeting with your students."

I rose to leave; Trip cleared his throat, saying, "Actually, I have something else to ask you, Maggie." I sat back down, and he continued, "I hope I am not off base, but I need a dinner companion for the March of Dimes fundraiser ball that is being held at this hotel a week from Saturday. I already have the tickets, but as I am relatively new in town, I do not know many single women I would consider asking, other than you. Oh, and by the way, it is a formal Black tie." Indeed, not the most flattering offer I have ever had, but I understood his dilemma.

The Black tie clinched it; I love attending gala events. Trying not to sound too eager, I cheerfully responded, "I would be happy to help you out."

Returning home, I read Trip's email; ten o'clock was one of the times he had listed. I sent an email to the five students assigned to the River Town Hotel project advising them about the Friday 10 a.m. meeting at the River Town Hotel, copying Trip so he would know to reserve that time.

I had not heard from anyone representing PSU Media Relations, I still wasn't sure how to broach the subject of Hannah's death with the group ... or with the rest of my students for that matter, so I made no mention of it in my email. I would have some explaining to do tomorrow to my Thursday afternoon students. Two of those students were also enrolled in the Services Marketing Course and were part of the group of five involved in the River Town Hotel Project. I sure hope I hear from the PSU spokesperson today.

In addition to my two face-to-face classes that meet on Mondays, I also teach a Front Desk Management class on Thursdays between 2 p.m. and 4:30 p.m. and an online course. All my courses contain online components, quizzes, case study discussions, weekly assignments, and the grade book for each class. Thus, I spend a considerable amount of time working from my home office.

Before I began teaching, I had no idea how much time and energy it took to prepare for each class! I planned on spending the rest of the afternoon and evening responding to comments in the group discussion forums, grading the previous week's quizzes, and preparing next week's introduction for the opening module for the online course.

Just as I suspected, my phone was ringing nonstop all afternoon. I resorted to screening my calls, letting most of them go to voicemail. I was relieved when I finally received the anticipated call from Susan Crenshaw, Executive Director of Institutional Communications for PSU. Susan asked me to explain the chain of events that led to my finding Hannah Johnson's body at the River Town Hotel and Conference Center.

I went over Monday's events with her, beginning with leaving my briefcase in the boardroom. I revealed nothing about my feelings about Hannah's appearance or about Trip saying she was on his expendable list. Unless he would like to be on the list of possible murder suspects, he probably wouldn't be sharing that choice tidbit with anyone else either; was that a real possibility? I didn't know Trip very well, but I could not believe he was a killer. What motive would he have? He could fire her, or could he? Did she have a contract, and if so, what were the conditions surrounding termination?

My imagination was running away with me, again! I quickly dropped that thought—realizing that Susan was speaking to me, "I understand members of the press may be trying to contact you; please take any future calls from the press, but do not answer their questions; simply give them my name and phone number."

"What should I say to my students?"

Susan Crenshaw replied, "Admit you found the body and know nothing else."

"That's easy; I don't know anything else!"

I confess I was glad when the day finally ended. About 9 p.m., I took the phone off the hook and went to bed.

Chapter Seven

E xcept for the phone ringing nonstop, Thursday morning was uneventful. I did take some of the calls, providing reporters with Susan Crenshaw's telephone number. I spent the morning preparing for my afternoon class in between phone calls.

The class was uneventful, except as anticipated, the students were eager for news about the murder at the River Town Hotel and Conference Center. The students viewed me as a celebrity of sorts as I had found the body. I simply shared, "I had no idea what was happening other than the local police were investigating."

The start of another day, and I hadn't slept well once again. I kept mulling things over in my mind. For starters, the condition of the board room was curious. Had there been a physical altercation? If so, why would someone bother to cover Hannah up with the tablecloth? I sure wish I knew who had killed Hannah and why.

I rationalized that the window of opportunity to kill Hannah was between 10 a.m. and noon. But breaking that time down, the students and I had been in Meeting Room C right next door to Meeting Room D from 10 a.m. till about 10:15 a.m. I am sure we would have heard something. We returned to Meeting Room C well before 11 a.m., which left Meeting Room C empty for roughly thirty plus minutes. Arlene had finished her lecture, and the students and I had departed the room for the lobby around 11:45 a.m. I had returned to Meeting Room D to retrieve my briefcase just before noon and found the door closed. Thinking back, I realized Arlene had closed the door when she and I had left the room and joined Trip and Hannah in the hall.

When Arlene and I initially walked down the hallway to Meeting Room D, a sign reading, "meeting in progress," was posted on the door of Meeting Room B. I wasn't sure who was in that room and how long they had been there. I will continue being annoyed with myself for not checking the reader board that day. There were people in that meeting room already. Might anyone have heard something? All this was weighing heavily on my mind. I decided to run all this by Trip when I saw him on Friday. Hopefully, he would be willing to share anything he had found out from the detectives. He may also have learned something during the employee meeting. I wanted to know what had killed her—gun, knife, blunt object, etc.—not to mention who.

I am glad it is Friday, and this stressful week will be over soon. Today is the third day this week I will be spending time at the River Town Hotel and Conference Center. I was excited about seeing Trip again today, selfishly, to find out if he had any new information about Hannah's murder.

I went for a walk, ate breakfast, and headed for my closet. What to wear? I chose a bright yellow dress with a full skirt, Peter Pan collar, and long sleeves, smartly accentuated with a navy-blue belt. Gold hoop earrings and navy-blue pumps completed my outfit. I remembered Mom and me picking out this dress at Dillard's just before she got sick. She had smiled at me, saying, "I can't believe that collar is back in style. Sunny yellow is an outlook changer." Twirling in front of the mirror, I was satisfied that I had chosen wisely. After my basic makeup routine of eyeliner and lipstick, I was ready for whatever the day may bring; but hopefully, nothing like Monday had been.

I arrived at the River Town Hotel and Conference Center at 9:50 a.m. All five of the students assigned to the hotel project were already sitting in the lobby, scanning their cell phones, looking up expectantly, acknowledging my arrival. People arriving too early for meetings was always an issue when I was a GM. Either they sat in the lobby waiting for me for a long time, or I had to adjust my schedule to accommodate them. Neither is a good situation.

I was pleased to see they all dressed appropriately, in student terms, meaning no tank tops, jeans, or flip-flops. I approached the hotel's front desk and told the receptionist that we were all here to meet Mr. Evans. She told me to take a seat, and she would let him know we had arrived. I took a chair next to Kimberly, the group leader. Kimberly put her cell phone in her purse and proceeded to tell me that the students had all decided to meet at the university and drive over together, which explains why they were all here at one time. I figured they had arrived early, assuming I would too, hoping for a gossip session about Hannah's murder. All eyes were on me.

Trip showed up in the nick of time, and I was off the hook. I stood to greet him; the students followed suit. I introduced "Mr. Evans" to the students he hadn't already met, and he told us to follow him to Meeting Room D, the boardroom. I am pretty sure none of the students knew that the boardroom was the "scene of the crime," and I was not about to tell them that.

Entering the room, I looked warily around for signs that a murder had taken place here a few days ago. The coffee and blood that had saturated a section of carpeting were no longer visible. The carpet had either been cleaned or replaced. Trip invited us to sit down. The students and I sat in chairs on either side of the table. Trip took command of the meeting, sitting in a high back chair at one end of the table.

I pulled a pad of paper, and a file folder from my briefcase, opened the file folder and distributed copies of today's meeting plan. I had attached the agenda to an email I sent Trip earlier that morning. I noticed he had it in front of him with pencil notations in the margin.

Trip would provide the students with an overview of the hotel's history, the importance of overcoming negative perceptions of the hotel, and recap the hotel's current vision and mission statements. We also needed to establish a timeline for the project.

Trip began the meeting by providing a condensed overview of the hotel's history, including tidbits about the previous owners. He emphasized how the hotel had been owned and operated for the past five years by a couple with no hotel experience. They had pocketed the profits and allowed the property to fall into disrepair. He told us that the hotel was now under new ownership; he was under contract to manage the hotel and had overseen the final stages of the extensive renovations. With the upgrades completed, he was in the process of building a new management team. He and Hannah, Director of Sales and Marketing, had already implemented a plan to disseminate ownership/management information to former guests.

He then remarked, "We had also been working on a marketing plan to attract new business. Hannah was murdered in the hotel last Monday, and Hannah's untimely death is sure to add to the hotel's negativity problem."

It was noteworthy that he didn't tell the students he intended to fire Hannah; not impugning her reputation after her death was a thoughtful, kind thing to do.

Trip went on to say, "The hotel switchboard is having a hard time keeping up with incoming phone calls: a few fearful people calling to cancel reservations, some wanting to make reservations, while other callers were just gossip seekers. Local reporters are showing up uninvited, hoping for a scoop to increase their paper's readership."

He segued into the topic, "overcoming negative perceptions of the hotel," telling the students about his employee meeting. His employees were given instructions not to enter into any conversations with reporters and make sure he knew when anyone from the press arrived; he would personally deal with them.

He had given every employee a copy of a short, upbeat statement they were to use when questioned about the hotel's new ownership or the murder. He handed the students a copy of the statement saying, if asked, please use this yourself—direct anyone seeking more information to contact me through the Front Desk.

At that point, I interjected, "Trip, customer interaction with employees was critical to changing the narrative. This project entails students interviewing the hotel's guests to obtain feedback about their satisfaction with employee services. Critical points of interaction between guests and employees, "moments of truth," would need assessment. Students will be making recommendations in their final reports about improving guest satisfaction."

I couldn't help worrying a bit, this project is a huge responsibility, and it is my job to make sure these students handle this correctly.

Trip covered the remaining items on the agenda, and the meeting lasted a little over an hour. We all agreed to meet at the hotel at the same time the following Friday. The students departed, enthused with the project but eager to start their weekend activities!

Trip asked, "Do you have time for coffee?"

I eagerly accepted. I could use a cup. I followed Trip to the restaurant, and he motioned to a seat at a window table for two. Given the time, there was no one else in the dining room. Trip excused himself, saying, "I will arrange for coffee service; be back in a minute." I watched him return carrying a tray containing a coffee pot, cups, saucers, spoons, and a cream pitcher and then proceed to set up our table, pouring us each a cup of coffee. I added sweetener and cream to mine.

Looking over the rim of my coffee cup, I smiled and offered, "You did a great job bringing the students up to date on the hotel's situation. Any news you can share about Hannah's murder? Have the police found the killer or the murder weapon yet?"

Trip looked at me thoughtfully before replying, "The police detectives still do not have a lead on the killer; just a large list of disgruntled people so far."

Taking a sip of his coffee, he continued, "I did learn that Hannah was stabbed several times with a knife. The knife might have come from the hotel kitchen. Kitchen knives are only accessible to people who have permission to be there, so that might cut the list of suspects down somewhat."

I decided to run my timeline by Trip to see what he thought.

"A roughly thirty-minute window between when we left Meeting Room C for the tour and returned to Meeting Room C for the lecture sounds about right to me, Maggie. In Hannah's absence, I was doing the quality assurance checks and met with the person who had booked the meeting in Meeting Room B.

I was pleased to learn the meeting went well; the room was perfect, and they loved the renovations.

However, very interesting, she did tell me that somewhere around 10:30 a.m., shortly after their coffee break ended, they had heard faint noises that sounded like dishes breaking coming from one of the rooms down the hall. I apologized for the distraction, and the meeting planner dismissed it, saying, "Not to worry, the noise hadn't lasted long, so it wasn't an issue."

Trip looked at me, exclaiming, "Come to think of it, Maggie, I know the detectives did not interview anyone who attended the meeting in that room. They never asked me for the group's name or a list of the attendees. I should probably call one of those detectives and tell them that!" I asked him if he knew who was on the suspect list? "The detectives did not share that with me, but there are a large number of people who might be, including me, Maggie." He laughingly retorted, "I would not be surprised to learn that I am on the top of that list."

"Ah, but you couldn't have killed her, Trip. You were with me during that window of time. We are each other's alibi. And Trip, if it turns out to be a knife from the kitchen, we can narrow it down to who may have been able to take it from the kitchen."

Trip looked at me, scolding, "Perhaps *we* should let the police department do its job." The sharpness of his reply caught me off guard. I had to admit, he certainly had more than enough to contend with without trying to figure out who had killed Hannah, and I told him that.

Trip took a deep breath looked at me soulfully, offering an apology, "I am so sorry, Maggie, I should not have spoken to you like that. I know you are only trying to help. I don't want to mess up the investigation by second-guessing the police department."

Whew, that was a tense moment! I decided to leave it at that and rose from my chair, saying, "Thanks for the coffee, Trip. We should get back to work." Trip walked me back to the lobby; we parted ways, and I left the Hotel with a quick nod at the desk clerk.

Before I left the house this morning, I had decided to visit Sara Milligan's shop, Dress for Success, after my meeting with Trip and the students. The March of Dimes ball is a week from tomorrow, and I was hoping Sara's shop carried formal dresses. The Dress for Success shop was close by and took only a few minutes to get there. I pulled into the parking lot, parked my car, and walked to the shop's front door.

The storefront windows contained mannequins dressed in stylish clothing geared toward fall weather, dark-colored pantsuits, skirts, and beautiful knit sweaters. An old-fashioned bell hanging over the door tinkled my arrival as I entered the shop. Greeting me was Sara, who seemed glad to see me, but I am a potential customer; why wouldn't she be?

After exchanging pleasantries, I told Sara I was looking for a formal dress to wear to the March of Dimes Ball next week. Remembering the strange look she had given me on Wednesday when I told her Trip, and I already knew each other, I opted not to say I was going with Trip.

Sara's shop boasted a large assortment of exquisite formal dresses. I tried on at least six dresses and finally settled on a long, fitted, off-white silk gown. One side of the dress had a small cap sleeve covered with multicolored sequins, and the other shoulder was bare. I brought my find to the cash register. Sara was in the process of checking out a customer. I waited my turn and studied Sara as she rang up their sale.

Sara wore a simple black pantsuit and a white blouse. It was hard not to notice the gorgeous jewel brooch adorning the lapel of her jacket or her sparkly diamond earrings, obviously multiple carats and expensive. I couldn't help admiring her trendy haircut, and her nails painted blood red. A blue sapphire ring encircled her right ring finger.

During our get-to-know-each-other conversation at the Rotary Club luncheon, Sara informed me she was single with no mention of being attached to anyone. It suddenly dawned on me that Sara and Trip knew each other; why hadn't he asked her to the ball? Sara was attractive, presented herself well, and was a business owner. I was curious but would never be bold enough to ask Trip or mention it to Sara!

Sara rang up my purchase, assuring me that all her formal dresses were one of a kind, meaning, hopefully, I would not be seeing anyone else at the ball with the same gown. She carefully placed it in a plastic garment bag emblazoned with the shop's logo.

Sara hesitated before handing me the garment bag and my copy of the sales slip, cautiously saying, "Maggie, I wanted to say something to you on Wednesday about Hannah's murder but thought it was not a good time to bring it up. I watched the 6 p.m. news on Tuesday and realized when you told me you had taken your students on a field trip to the hotel on Monday that you were the one who found Hannah's body. That must have been an awful experience."

"Yes; indeed, it had been me. Thank you for your concern."

Sara then asked, "Is the killer in jail yet?"

"I don't know, but I hope so."

"Maggie, I knew Hannah; we went to high school together and lived in River Town most of our lives. We were never friends, traveling in different social circles, but I am sorry that Hannah's life came to such an abrupt horrible end."

I quietly asked, "Do you have any idea who might have wanted Hannah dead?"

Sara stared at me for a minute before admitting, "Not really, but I did hear rumors about Hannah's involvement in a ruckus at a local bar recently. I don't want to further the gossip, especially now that Hannah is dead."

"Do you think you should tell the police?"

Sara way to quickly replied, "I do not want to become involved in a murder investigation; not good for business, you know—but I will think about it."

After talking to Sara about Hannah, I left the shop with my initial delight in finding a dress for the ball somewhat dampened. Having no plans to go anywhere else, I drove home, mulling over in my mind what Sara had confided. What wasn't Sara willing to say about the unrest at the bar? You don't think much happens in small towns, but something must have happened here. I wasn't quite sure how to find out about that "ruckus."

When the phone rang, I was treating myself to an afternoon of light reading, a wonderful who done it mystery by Janet Evanovich.

I was surprised to hear Trip's voice; I wasn't expecting him to call. Trip told me he had been in a glum mood all day and was sorry to have lashed out at me about investigating Hannah's death. He hesitantly told me; he suddenly realized his job could be at stake. The police department hadn't had much success. Helping me was the right thing to do, but he didn't want to discuss Hannah's death over the phone and asked me to meet him at the hotel on Monday at 9:30 a.m. I agreed, and we hung up.

My wheels were spinning. Perhaps Trip had heard the gossip about Hannah; I must remember to ask him on Monday.

The weekend was routine, filled with household chores, grocery shopping, and preparing for courses the following week. I must admit I was excited about meeting Trip on Monday, eager to find out what he knew. To be honest, I was looking forward to seeing him again. Every time we meet, more and more about Trip Evans comes to light. Monday morning couldn't get here soon enough.

Chapter Eight

Monday, the beginning of a new work week; ironically, this Monday is starting just like last Monday. I would be meeting with Trip at the hotel first thing in the morning. Hopefully, there will be no murders or other unpleasant events happening today. I couldn't help thinking about how much had changed in just one short week—Hannah's death, my growing friendship with Trip, and a Black tie event to look forward to on Saturday.

Arriving at the hotel five minutes before my 9:30 a.m. meeting, greeting me by name was the same receptionist staffing the front desk last Monday. Glancing at her name tag, I replied by greeting Angela by name. I was pleased that she had recognized me. But then, hospitality employees are trained to remember the names of hotel guests and business people who frequent the hotel.

Angela told me that Trip was expecting me and provided directions to his office. I set out to find him; only after I checked out the hotel reader board proving I could learn from my mistakes. Not much is happening at the hotel today, only a few small meetings.

Trip's office was easy to find. The door to his office was open. I hesitated at the entrance; sensing my presence, he looked up, invited me in, and came around the desk to greet me. Trip led me to a sitting area in the office and motioned to sit at a small conference table. I suddenly felt a little awkward. Glancing sideways at him, I thought he might be feeling the same.

Trip spoke first, thanking me for coming in to meet him. Getting right into the reason I was here, discussing Hannah's murder, he admitted, "I do not have much to tell you, but I will try to answer questions you may have."

I thanked him and cut through the chase, asking, "Any news about the knife?"

"Yes, employees had been questioned, separately, by the detectives on the day of the murder. Chef Louie had also spoken to every member of his kitchen staff when he returned to work the following day.

"The best anyone could come up with was no one had noticed any knives missing, but then they work with so many knives, why would they? After the autopsy, there may be more information about the type of knife used to kill Hannah."

"Trip, have any of the employees been able to shed any light on who might be unhappy enough with Hannah to wish her harm?"

"More than one employee told me, 'There were too many to count!'"

It dawned on me that perhaps a disgruntled guest may be the murderer, and I told Trip so.

"Good point, Maggie; I am in the process of reviewing all the recent contracts and event comment cards to see if anything jumps out; nothing has surfaced to date."

Next, I told Trip about my recent conversation with Sara Milligan while buying a dress at her shop. Sara said she knew Hannah, and they both had been residents of River Town all their lives; they attended high school together.

"I did not know that, but I have no reason to believe they were friends or enemies, for that matter. I have never seen them at the hotel or anywhere else together."

I told him what Sara had voiced about them not traveling in the same social circle.

"I didn't think they would."

"Trip, Sara also brought up the subject of Hannah's murder. She told me she had heard rumors about Hannah's involvement with locals at a bar. However, Sara did not want to tell me what the stories were. I suggested she contact the police, and her only commitment was, 'She would think about it.'"

"I hadn't heard about that," Trip said, "I will ask around in case any of my employees have heard any rumors."

Sitting there, thinking, I suddenly had an inspiration. "Trip, have you checked Hannah's personnel file to see if there were any disputes or perhaps reprimands that might be a reason for someone to dislike her, enough to want her dead?"

"I reviewed all personnel files when I first arrived here, but that was a while ago. I wouldn't have looked for anything specific and could have overlooked an employee dispute. We can do that right now. I happen to have those files in my office."

Trip walked over to a tall filing cabinet to the right of his desk, taking a set of keys out of a desk drawer, unlocked a file drawer from which he pulled a relatively thick file. He began to skim through the pages, and after a few minutes, he looked up at me, smirked, and gleefully announced, "pay dirt!"

Trip pulled out a newspaper article dated several months before his arrival at the hotel. Reading through the article, it seems that several of the hotel's employees were suspects in connection with the previous hotel owner's complaint about missing cash and misused credit cards. Ironically, we found no mention of Hannah's name.

"Confusing, but Trip, don't you think that article was in her file for a reason?"

Trip agreed, speculating, "Perhaps Hannah knew these employees, and the previous owners thought she was involved or could shed some light on the situation."

I asked Trip if any of the employees mentioned in the article were still working at the hotel?

"Yes, one person still works here, and some of the other names are familiar. I will double-check our payroll records and check all their personnel files to see what else may turn up."

Glancing at my watch, it was now 11 a.m. "I really must go, Trip, and I am sure you have a lot to do today as well."

He nodded, saying, "I think we may be on to something here, but I don't want to involve the police unless we have something concrete to pass along."

"I heartily agree!"

Trip concluded, saying, "I will begin reviewing the personnel files and anticipate having that done by Friday."

"I will check out the library to look for more newspaper articles about the hotel's missing money and misused credit cards."

We decided to take a few minutes on Friday after the Marketing Class meeting to exchange notes.

Trip rose from his chair, saying, "I will walk you out."

I was going to protest but thought, why?

On our way back to the lobby, Trip enthusiastically announced, "I am looking forward to the March of Dimes Ball on Saturday."

I smiled to myself, looked up, and happily responded, "So am I; I hope you can dance?!"

"I love to dance, Ms. McManus, especially to music where you get to hold your partner close." I didn't respond, but corny as this may sound, I thought, "be still my heart."

Chapter Nine

Monday afternoon classes went without a hitch, except that some of the students taking the 2 p.m. class had arrived extra early, trying to rope me into talking about Hannah's murder. I changed the subject, telling them quickly that I was not involved in the investigation and was unaware of what was going on. Productive class time today; most of the students had read the assigned material and engaged in the classroom discussions. My 5 p.m. Services Marketing students had all met with their *community partners*; group projects were underway! I was looking forward to hearing about their progress the following week.

On my way home, I couldn't help thinking about how much my life had changed recently. I was no longer feeling lonely. I was developing a sense of belonging because of my memberships in the Chamber of Commerce and the Rotary Club. My students exude enthusiasm and an eagerness to learn and listen to the real-life stories I share from my experience working in the hospitality industry.

However, there has been a downside; last year, the River Town campus was ravaged by a hurricane, destroying sections of the College of Business Building, including the hospitality offices. I have been working from home ever since I started in August. I haven't had much personal interaction with my department chair or the other instructors yet. The people I have met have been friendly and willing to help me get acclimated to my new position, except for Professor Harrison.

Professor Harrison has gone out of his way to intimidate or belittle me, telling me that I should stay in the background and speak only when spoken to during faculty meetings since I was new to academic life. Funny, my Department Chair hadn't mentioned a word to me about that. I vowed that I would not allow Professor Harrison to get under my skin.

Wednesday. I attended the Rotary Club luncheon, and as I walked into the room, I saw Trip and Sara engaged in what appeared to be a serious conversation. Sara looked annoyed about something; Trip was shaking his head and trying to calm her down. I was curious about what could have caused her to be so upset. I am sure Trip will tell me at some point.

I decided not to approach Trip and Sara and joined a group of people sitting at a table. I was not lucky enough to escape recognition this week; as soon as I sat down, a distinguished elderly man to the right of me asked, "Aren't you the Instructor at PSU who found Hannah's body?" I admitted I was. He introduced himself as Tim Swank, Superintendent of Schools, asking me my name.

"Maggie McManus, and I am pleased to meet you, Tim."

Superintendent Swank proceeded to talk about the murder. Sharing he had known Hannah for many years, her death had come as a shock. He went on to say even though Hannah had been in trouble during her high school years, no one thought she would come to this.

I couldn't help asking, "What kind of trouble?"

Tim's off-hand reply, "Oh, the usual teenage stuff; underage drinking, hanging out with the wrong kind of boys; ran away from home once, but the police found her and brought her home. After graduating from high school, Hannah seemed to straighten out and even went to college."

Pausing briefly, Tim seemed to be weighing his subsequent remark, "Lately, though, there's been talk that those same boys from her high school days started harassing her."

"What were they harassing her about?"

"I don't know. Maggie, but even as grown men, they still represent trouble; let me put it this way; they are not unknown to the police department."

I would love to have asked him their names, but that might carry my curiosity too far. The meeting convened, and so our conversation ended.

Another excellent lunch—Beef Stroganoff with buttered noodles, steamed carrots, assorted rolls, and a delicious baked apple dessert with whipped cream.

After lunch, everyone at our table remained silent: seemingly, intently listening as Robert Wilson, Rotary Club President, addressed the items on the meeting agenda. The final article for discussion was a fundraiser to provide college scholarships for high school students graduating in the spring. Of course, I was delighted to hear that.

After much debate, President Wilson decided to form a committee to research fundraising ideas, asking, "By a show of hands, who is interested in serving on the committee?" Tim and I raised our hands, as did four other people sitting at various tables in the room. The president noted our names. Looking over his list of volunteers, President Wilson singled out Tim, asking, "Would you be willing to chair the committee?"

"Yes, of course."

"Thanks, Tim— I will provide you with the names and phone numbers of the new committee members."

The meeting adjourned. I stood up and, with a quick goodbye to Tim and my tablemates, whose names I didn't know, I headed for the front door of the hotel, looking around on my way out for Trip and Sara; they were nowhere in sight.

Chapter Ten

I was up early Friday morning, eager to begin the day. Temperatures in River Town, this time of year, are around sixty degrees. Reminiscent of a typical fall day in New England, perfect for morning walks. I set off at 7:30 a.m., and by the time I returned home, I was ready for my first cup of coffee and a quick breakfast of raisin toast and cornflakes with low-fat two percent milk sprinkled with sweetener.

After taking a long hot shower and washing and drying my hair, I dressed casually in a pair of brown slacks, a crème-colored cable knit sweater, and brown low-riser boots. I applied makeup and affixed my gold Claddagh earrings, an excellent match for today's Irish-inspired outfit.

Today at 10 a.m., I will be attending a second meeting with Trip and the group of Services Marketing students involved in a project at the River Town Hotel and Conference Center.

The River Town Hotel is a large facility, and customer contact happens in many areas: front desk, housekeeping, maintenance, restaurant, meeting rooms, and banquets.

Students will be working with Trip to develop a blueprint that would identify the various contact points between guests and hotel employees — in hospitality speak, "moments of truth," which are any interaction during which a customer may form an impression of your brand or product. This impression may be either positive or negative.

It would take several sessions to complete this phase of their project.

Again today, Angela was behind the front desk and greeted me warmly as soon as I walked in, saying, "Nice to see you, Maggie. Trip wants you and the students to go to the boardroom; he will meet you there."

"Thanks, Angela; I will round them up and head over there."

The students were clustered together in the lobby, sitting quietly, staring at their cell phones, fingers tapping rapidly over the keypads, looking up briefly before echoing a greeting as they saw me approaching. I told them to gather their belongings and follow me that Trip was waiting for us in the boardroom.

The students worked with Trip and me for over an hour. Once they understood the concept, they breezed through today's assignment to identify contact points for several of the hotel departments, surprising themselves at the considerable progress they made in such a short time. Gathering their papers from the table, the students left with choruses of, "Have a nice weekend, Professor McManus and Mr. Evans."

We both chimed in, wishing them the same.

Thursday morning, I had gone to the library to look for updates to the newspaper article Trip had found in Hannah's personnel file. Much to my disappointment, there weren't any, or at least that I could find; asking the librarian for assistance might have helped, but I did not want to bring any undue attention to myself. Well, I could at least share with Trip what the Superintendent of Schools had to say about Hannah.

I was eager to learn if Trip had found anything in the hotel's personnel files.

After the students departed, Trip suggested we go to his office, saying, "I found out some interesting things about Hannah that I want to run by you."

I picked up my briefcase and followed him to his office. We settled into the same seats we had occupied Monday morning. Trip opened the file lying on the table and picked up a typewritten paper from the top of the small stack of papers inside.

Studying me for my reaction, Trip said, "I began to realize that there were far too many facts and ideas running through my head to keep everything straight. I decided I had better start documenting what I was learning about Hannah and her murder."

"Great idea; I am beginning to feel overwhelmed; I should do that myself!"

"Well, here is something else to boggle our minds, Maggie! I had an opportunity to ask several employees about Hannah. It seems that Hannah Johnson was a distant relative of the hotel's original owner, James Johnson. Although Hannah had no monetary interest in the hotel, she made no bones about telling people, usually rather snootily, that she was related. No doubt, she felt this gave her job security, and she could pretty much do what she wanted, probably the reason so many employees disliked her. I can't imagine what would have transpired when the time came to fire her."

Thinking about that for a minute, from a psychological standpoint, I ventured to say, "Hannah must have been a pretty insecure person to measure her self-worth through the lens of a distant genealogical connection."

Trip, said, "Very astute of you, Maggie, and sadly I have to agree. I spoke to one of the men mentioned in the article, the only one who still works here. He told me the police had interviewed him about the missing money and misuse of credit cards; he claims innocence, saying nothing that he knew of ever came of it. I asked him about Hannah, and he acknowledged knowing who she was and guessed that someone had it in for her. I asked him if anyone special came to mind? He told me there was no one in particular; she was not well-liked."

Trip finished by saying, "I checked the personnel files of the employees mentioned in the article who are no longer here. Their files contained nothing to indicate termination for cause; everyone left at different times for personal reasons."

Mulling this over, I asked, "Trip, do you think this is a dead-end? Any word yet on what kind of knife killed Hannah?"

"Not sure about a dead-end, Maggie, and nothing from the medical examiner about the knife, or at least nothing they are telling me. I do have a little more information to share, though. I remembered you expressing concern about Sara being unwilling to share local gossip about Hannah with you and decided to ask her myself.

"I spoke to Sara about that at the Rotary Club meeting on Wednesday. I saw you come in out of the corner of my eye but didn't want to acknowledge you and miss the opportunity to continue speaking with Sara. I asked her how well she knew Hannah and what she thought could motivate someone to want her dead? That's when she told me about the gossip.

"Hannah, it seems, was recently seen drinking at a local bar with two men known to be in and out of trouble with the law. There was a confrontation between Hannah and the two men. The police showed up; Hannah went home, but the two men ended up at the police station for questioning. I asked if she knew what the confrontation was about or who the men were? 'Although no one mentioned their names, she suspected they might be guys Hannah used to hang out with in high school.'"

I told Trip what Tim Swank, Superintendent of Schools, had shared about Hannah being in trouble in high school, especially about her associating with the wrong boys. Tim also told me, 'There is talk that those same boys from her high school days had started harassing her; he was unsure why.'

"Just a thought, but any of the men mentioned in the article might be involved in harassing her. I am on a committee with Tim, and we should be meeting soon. Perhaps I could find a way to run their names by him?"

Trip agreed and wrote their names on a piece of paper. Handing me the paper, he cautioned, "Be careful. You don't want to jeopardize your career or your life."

That seemed to be all we had to discuss relative to the murder. The subject of the dance the following evening was next. Trip offered to pick me up, but I said I would meet him at the Hotel. Reiterating, "I know from experience, hotel managers can be somewhat undependable, having been one of those unreliable people myself. We are often held hostage just waiting for a crisis to end."

We both laughed and agreed it would be best if we came and went on our own.

"Do you know what color dress you will be wearing yet?"

"Yes, I do, off-white with multicolored sequins."

To which he did not comment, just grinned. He escorted me to the front door, waved goodbye, saying, "See you tomorrow; be sure to wear comfortable shoes for dancing."

Chapter Eleven

I spent Saturday morning enmeshed in my weekly house-keeping chores, happy to have them out of the way, free-ing up my weekend. Freshly showered and dressed in casual clothes, I slid into the driver's seat of the Camaro and drove downtown to keep my hair and nail appointment at Elegant Tresses. At precisely 1 p.m., I entered the local spa and salon to have my hair washed and styled in an elegant updo. I had decided to splurge on a French manicure and a pedicure. These elaborate preparations took the better part of the afternoon.

I was to meet Trip at the hotel at 6 p.m. and commenced dressing at 5 p.m. I stepped into my exquisite off-white, floor-length sheath with its one brightly colored sequined short sleeve. Reaching around, I carefully zipped up the back of the dress, never an easy task. I fastened a necklace around my neck that perfectly matched the colors of the sequins on my gown. After adding companion earrings, carefully applying lipstick, eye shadow, and mascara, I slipped on pantyhose and a pair of off-white satin shoes. Placing Kleenex, makeup, driver's license, credit card, and a small amount of cash for tips in a matching satin purse, I was ready.

Slipping on a short off-white faux fur jacket, I felt like Cinderella as I headed off to the March of Dimes Ball; the only thing missing was the coach and horses.

Glancing around the lobby, Trip was nowhere in sight, so I checked my jacket with the hotel's cloakroom attendant, who directed me to sign in at the ballroom entrance. Arlene was greeting people at the door and checking names off the guest list. She looked up as I approached the table, saying, "Wow, you look fantastic, Maggie! I hope you have an enjoyable evening."

After thanking her, I began scrutinizing the ballroom. The setup was a combination of eight and ten top tables, beautifully appointed with crisp white linen tablecloths. White base plates with wide gold rims and the hotel's logo etched with gold and black in the center were placed on the table in front of each seat. Pale blue napkins, folded in an elegant fan fold, were placed on the base plates.

Indicative of a multi-course dinner, silverware was placed on either side and at the top of the base plates. Coffee cups and saucers, two crystal wine glasses, and one water glass were appropriately set to the right of each place setting; matching bread and butter plates were placed on the left.

A spectacular, tall, colorful fresh floral centerpiece, obviously arranged by a professional florist, was placed in the center of each table. Two sets of crystal salt and pepper shakers, a crystal sugar caddy, and plates of heart-shaped pats of butter were placed strategically on either side of the table.

Now, I must admit most people would not have scrutinized the room or table setting so carefully. Hospitality professionals, however, are conditioned to take note of everything, right down to the name tags resting to the top left of each base plate.

Still looking around for Trip, a smiling, tuxedo-clad server carrying a tray of champagne flutes approached me. I selected a glass from the tray and made my way toward a long hors d'oeuvres table set up on one side of the room; I had reached the hors d'oeuvres line when Trip arrived at my side carrying a flower box.

Moving away from the hors d'oeuvres table, Trip opened the box containing a brightly colored floral wrist corsage and fastened them to my left wrist. I couldn't believe how perfectly the colors matched the sequins on my dress and told him so.

"Now, Maggie, I knew anyone who dared to leave home wearing a bright yellow dress that would give the bumblebees a run for their money would not be wearing pink and blue pastels. When I asked you about your dress color, I knew those sequins you mentioned contained bright yellow and purple. And by the way, I love your dress; you look beautiful!"

"Thank you. I bought the dress at Sara's store." The admiring way he was looking at me caused me to blush.

With that, Trip sighed, "I guess now would be a good time to tell you something I should have told you a while ago.

Let me get some champagne, and we can go someplace quiet so that I can fill you in."

We stopped by the bar; Trip deposited the flower box in a trash receptacle and picked up a champagne bottle and a glass. Leading me into the meeting room next door, we sat down at a table. Trip popped the champagne cork, refreshed my drink, and poured one for himself. Studying my face as he took his first sip of champagne, he began, "This is about Sara and me, Maggie."

I waited with my hands folded in my lap while Trip gathered his thoughts, hoping I would be able to handle whatever his news might be!

"When I first moved to River Town, I met Sara at a Chamber of Commerce meeting. She seemed pleasant enough, perhaps a little needy, but I was lonely and asked her out on a date. The way she latched on to me on that first date made me extremely nervous, and I never asked her out again. However, after that date, I unwisely accepted two invites from her to attend Chamber of Commerce Business Events, the last one being two months ago. I did not think she was right for me, or me for her, for that matter.

"Maggie, I have been actively avoiding her for months. Last Wednesday, I decided to tell Sara that I was taking you to the ball. She flipped out, accusing me of leading her on and embarrassing her. At one point, she raised her hand as if to slap me but restrained herself. She began rambling about you stealing me away. I told her that you and I had never dated; my taking you to the ball was meant as a nice gesture. Sara lashed out, 'It didn't take you long to make a move. Maggie told me she met you on Monday, and by Wednesday, she is your date for the gala of the year. You had no thoughts about me.'"

Trip continued, carefully watching my face for a reaction, "Maggie, I am telling you this because I am concerned; Sara is hurt and angry looking to blame someone; she might do something spiteful to punish you or me or both of us."

I reached across the table for Trip's hand, and he covered my hand with his. "I appreciate your concern and for telling me this, Trip. When you told me you didn't know anyone to ask to the ball, I later wondered why you had not considered Sara; you had known her for a while, and she is an attractive, intelligent woman. Now I understand that asking her to the ball would have meant continuing a relationship with no future and would have led her on from your perspective. Also, your attending without a date might have given her the impression she still had a chance."

Trip, still gently holding my hand, replied, "Maggie, I hadn't looked at it from that last perspective."

"Do you know if Sara is attending the ball?"

"Yes, she is. Arlene and I created a seating chart from the guest list, and I saw her name on it, which is why I needed to tell you right away. She will be sitting at a table for ten purchased by a local banker."

"Well, Trip, hopefully, those bankers will be a diversion for her. And by the way, I am honored you asked me to the ball; that was a very thoughtful gesture."

My sense of humor got the best of me, and I chuckled, "As long as we don't find another dead body, it ought to be an enjoyable evening!"

Trip chimed in, "We'll stay close together, with Sara on the warpath; I don't want to worry about finding yours this evening. Shall we join the festivities?"

Returning my hand, Trip placed the cork back in the champagne bottle; with his left hand on the bottle, he extended his right arm. Looping my arm through his, Trip escorted me back to the ballroom.

Chapter Twelve

I t so seems we needn't worry about Sara creating a scene. Her assigned seat at the table remained vacant all evening. Early in the evening, Trip decided to ask Harold Thorpe, the banker who had invited Sara, if he knew what had happened to her? Harold admitted, "I don't. I am as mystified as you are. Sara verified her attendance with my secretary on Thursday afternoon." Trip and I both found that rather odd and agreed that Trip taking me to the ball probably wouldn't have been enough to dissuade her from attending. Sara wouldn't have missed the ball unless there was something wrong. As there wasn't anything we could do about Sara now, Trip and I decided to enjoy the evening and figure out what happened to Sara later.

Dinner was sumptuous! Beginning with the spectacular array of appetizers that we finally got to enjoy, followed by a sit-down dinner of lobster bisque, Caesar salad, crescent rolls, and the main course, Surf and Turf - lobster tail and filet mignon; the desert was a flaming banana forester. No better way to enjoy such a fabulous meal than to share it with a group of delightful table mates handpicked by Trip, professionals actively involved in making River Town a great place to live and work. Trip told me he knew them all personally.

He introduced me to Todd and Jennifer Davis, real estate agents who had sold Trip his house, Bart Flanagan, the River Town Hotel and Conference Center's lawyer, and his wife Glenda, a River Town elementary school teacher. The last couple was River Town's Mayor, Ralph Scott, and his wife, Clara, a former River Town librarian. Clara was now a stay-at-home mother to their five children ranging from three to twelve.

I was seated next to Jennifer. We hit it off immediately. Jennifer told me she and Todd were originally from Maine and transplanted to River Town about twenty years ago; they couldn't take the snow anymore but loved fall, making the Panhandle of Florida a perfect place for them. Their three children were grown up, married, and still living in the Panhandle.

I told Jennifer I had never been married, close once, but just not the right person in the end. She asked me about my family, and I told her I was an only child and that my parents were both deceased. She empathetically replied, "Sorry to hear that, Maggie."

I was glad she didn't linger on that subject. Instead, she moved on to tell me about how up-and-coming River Town was and share how much she loved selling real estate. Jennifer then asked, "How do you like your new job?"

I gave her a rundown on the student's recent projects, including working with the River Town Hotel and Conference Center. She told me she and Todd loved Trip; they considered him family. Trip spent as much time as he could with them. I would like to have asked her about Trip's own family but thought better of it. He would tell me what he wanted me to know when he was ready.

The band began playing, and Trip turned his attention away from Mayor Scott, with whom he had been animatedly chatting, back to me.

Everyone at our table rose at once, making their way to the dance floor. Trip took me in his arms, smiling down at me, placed his right hand on my waist and his left hand in my right hand. Looking him in the eyes, I smiled up at him and responded by putting my left hand on Trip's right shoulder, and we began to glide effortlessly in step to a beautiful rendition of "You Light up My Life."

Trip, I discovered, knew all the proper steps to the Waltz, Fox Trot, Rumba, and Salsa, telling me he had taken ballroom dancing lessons. Much to his delight, I told him so had I. We danced perfectly in step, and when variations in tempo warranted it, we quickly changed dance styles. We stopped by many of the tables between dance sets to introduce ourselves. Trip presented me as a hospitality instructor at PSU and himself as the hotel's general manager asking everyone we talked to if they had enjoyed their dinner … a nostalgic reminder of my hotel days as a GM.

The bandleader, all too soon, from my point of view, announced that the next song would be the last. Trip held me tight as we danced to the beautiful, appropriate tune, "The Last Waltz." People started leaving immediately after that. Trip and

I walked to the cloakroom hand in hand. I retrieved my jacket, and Trip held my coat for me while I slipped into it.

Walking me outside to my car, he waited while I recovered my car keys from my purse. Taking them from me, Trip unlocked my car door. Before opening it, he solemnly said, "Maggie, this has been one of the best evenings I have had in a very long time." I was glad it was dark out, so he wouldn't catch me blushing for a second time this evening.

I thanked him for inviting me, adding, "I had a lovely time; I thoroughly enjoyed the food, the music, the ambiance, and the opportunity to dance again!"

I slid into the car, closed the door, and waved goodbye. Chivalry is not a lost art after all, and I uttered aloud, "What a guy!"

When I arrived home, there was a short message from Sara on my cell phone, "Call me as soon as possible; I have something important to tell you." The recorded time was 5:10 p.m. I must have been in the bedroom, getting ready for the ball, when she left me that message. I admonished myself, "To do a better job checking my cell phone for messages."

If what she had to tell me was so important, why hadn't she come to the ball knowing I would be there? Unless what she wanted to talk about was Trip. Still odd that she would forgo attending the dance and leave me a phone message. My gut told me to call Trip before I called her back tomorrow; well, I would sleep on it and see if my *gut changed its mind.*

Chapter Thirteen

I decided to call Trip before calling Sara back. I waited until 9 a.m. and dialed his office. I was relieved when he answered. Hearing his voice, I suddenly became tongue-tied unsure how to proceed. I finally just blurted out, "Sara left me a telephone message last night at 5:10 p.m. She mentioned she had something important to tell me. I haven't returned her call yet. I was wondering if, by any chance, she left you a message?"

"She didn't, Maggie, and I am worried that she might have something evil up her sleeve; if she asks, please do not meet with her alone." Pausing briefly, Trip thoughtfully asked, "Would you feel more comfortable having me present when you call her back? I don't think it would be a good idea to place it from my phone, and we certainly wouldn't want her to know I was listening in. How about I come over to your house while you place the call?"

I gratefully accepted, humbly adding, "Much appreciated."

"I will be over at 11 a.m., Maggie. I need to place a few 'courtesy calls' to hotel guests before I am free for the day." I gave him directions to my house, thankful that he was coming over to support me.

My house is a small but charming craftsman bungalow. I was pretty proud of the colorful fall flower beds I had recently planted bordering my manicured yard. I watched from the window as Trip parked his car in the driveway. He stood in the driveway surveying the front of my house before he climbed the three front steps, boasting a pot of pansies on each riser, leading up to an inviting covered front porch. I had positioned two matching rocking chairs with floral cushions in one corner and a wooden glider in the other, creating an attractive and practical entry to my home.

I waited until he rang the bell before opening the front door. Trip stepped into my house, looking appreciatively around at the large open floor plan encompassing living, kitchen, and dining. A wall-to-wall fireplace is the focal point of the room. I had placed matching plaid sofas across from each other in front of the fireplace and decorated the space with live plants, floral arrangements, throw pillows, and books. A dining room table and six chairs filled the ample space between the kitchen and living area.

After openly studying the room, trip said, "Wow, Maggie, your house looks like something straight out of HGTV Magazine. I love your modern kitchen with its tall white kitchen cabinets, stainless steel appliances, and granite countertops. Your home is not only beautiful; it feels warm and inviting."

I thanked him, saying, "I am happy you like it! It is quite different from the other homes I have lived in, but I enjoy living here."

Gesturing to a seat at the dining room table, I offered Trip coffee or a cold drink. He declined the offer, and I sat down across from him. Trip openly concerned asked, "Are you OK?"

I nervously replied, "I am worried about getting into a confrontation with Sara."

"My best suggestion is, if the call becomes uncomfortable, hang up. You don't owe Sara anything; you don't even have to call her back unless you want to."

Sighing heavily, before admitting, "I know, Trip, but I am concerned that she may have information about Hannah's murder, and I would hate to miss that."

I picked up my cell phone and dialed Sara's cell phone number. After ten rings, Sara hadn't answered, and there were no instructions to leave a message. Looking quizzically at Trip, I asked, "By any chance, you don't happen to have a number other than her cell phone?"

"I have her home phone, Maggie," pulling out his cell phone to retrieve it.

"I hope Sara doesn't ask me where I got this number," I said as I dialed. Sara didn't answer, but at least, after six rings, the caller was instructed to "Leave a message after the beep."

"Sara, this is Maggie. I am returning your call from last evening. Please call me back." I hung up the phone and turned to Trip, "Now I am getting concerned. Do you have time to go for a ride with me? I want to see if her car is at her shop or her home?"

"Of course, I'll drive; let's go."

Sara's shop, revealing no signs of life, had a "closed on Sunday" sign on the door. I asked Trip if he knew what she drove and where she lived?

"I am pretty sure it is a red Buick Cascada, and her house is a few streets over from here."

It only took us a few minutes to get there. Trip pulled up in front of her house and parked the car. The blinds in the front windows were closed, and her car was not in the driveway.

"If she is home, the car could be in the garage," I offered. "What's next, Watson?"

A little levity was a welcome break, and chuckling Trip played along, saying, "I guess we could use some advice from Sherlock Holmes; sleuthing isn't easy!"

I took a moment to think things through. "You know, Trip, those detectives will laugh at us if we share our concern that Sara was acting a bit unhinged and missed the ball. So, I guess our only option is to search for her on our own."

"I don't know Sara well enough to have any insight into her Sunday routine, but we could cruise Main Street to see if she is at one of the local restaurants," Trip suggested?

"Or churches I offered. Given that Sara may not be missing, just a figment of our overactive minds, it would be helpful if we, at least, found her car in a public place."

We spent the next two hours driving around River Town, hoping for a *Sara sighting*. I checked my cell and home phone several times for messages; Sara had not left one. Shortly after 1:30 p.m., Trip suggested stopping at the hotel to see if anyone needed him. I was getting worn down by all this driving around and readily agreed.

It was a quiet day at the River Town Hotel and Conference Center; the front parking lot was pretty much empty, and so was the lobby, for that matter. The front desk receptionist told Trip that no one had stopped by the desk looking for him while he was out. Trip glanced through his messages and suddenly gasped, "Maggie, look at this!" It was a note from the daytime security guard regarding a red Buick Cascada parked in a no-parking spot at the rear of the hotel. It so seems that the evening security guard had placed a warning notice on the car late last night. The car was still there when the daytime security guard made his rounds at noon.

We exited the hotel on a mission to check the parking lot for ourselves. Sure enough, Sara's car turned up behind the hotel, and Sara wasn't in it. We now had a real good reason to worry that something might have happened to Sara.

Returning to the hotel lobby, after ensuring Sara had not checked into the hotel, we began a systematic search for her. I took the ladies' rooms and the meeting rooms on the ABCD wing, and Trip headed toward the dining room, meeting rooms, and ballroom in the other corridor. We agreed to meet in his office after we completed our search.

My first stop was the ladies' room off the lobby; I even checked the stalls, there was no one there. I made my way down the hallway, checking inside each meeting room as I went. Meeting room doors A, B, and C were all closed, and as I slowly opened each one of them, I noted the rooms were in some state of limbo, either being set up or torn down.

Meeting Room D, the infamous boardroom, was the last place on my list. I slowly opened the door and let out a scream. Sara was sitting in a chair, slumped over the table. I cautiously walked over to her; she didn't appear to be breathing. How could this be happening again? I took out my cell phone and called Trip's office, no answer, of course, he was still searching for Sara! I called the hotel's main number and told the receptionist to page Trip, and please tell him to come to the boardroom immediately!

Trip warily opened the door; I watched him enter the room, quickly closing the door when he saw Sara slumped over the table. Checking Sara for a pulse, finding none, he swore, "Oh no, what the Hell!" He walked over to the table and sat down next to me, saying, "You look pale as a ghost! Sorry for the profanity."

"Given the situation, Trip, it's forgivable!"

A repeat performance; we made sure the board room door was closed and locked with us inside; Trip called 911 and then the front desk to tell them that the boardroom was off-limits to everyone, except the police who were on their way.

Chapter Fourteen

While we sat waiting for the police, we looked around the room, making mental notes. It appears that Sara met someone here; before or after the ball, we had no way of knowing which. "Curiously though," I pointed out to Trip, "Sara is wearing formal attire, and her evening bag is sitting in her lap; it seems like she was planning on attending the ball. Her full-length fur coat draped across the back of her chair means she didn't have the time or desire to check it into the cloakroom." Across the table from Sara, an uncorked bottle of red wine sat next to a half-filled wine glass; an empty wine glass was sitting in front of Sara.

"So," Trip asked in disbelief, "what could have caused Sara's death? She doesn't appear physically assaulted; perhaps she had a heart attack?"

"If Security checked these rooms during their nightly patrol, why hadn't they seen Sara's body and called someone," I asked? I didn't want to upset Trip, so I didn't say out loud what came to my mind; maybe the security guard should be on the same expendable list Hannah was!

Trip cut short our speculation, saying, "The police should be here soon; no doubt both of us will be asked what we were doing in the boardroom?"

"I don't think it is a good idea to lie to them, Trip, but if they don't ask, we shouldn't volunteer anything."

Trip suggested we tell them about touring River Town to acquaint you with the area. The fact that we were driving around town looking for Sara would not bode well and open us up to further questioning.

"Also, the truth of the matter is," Trip contended, "I was following up on a Security report that Sara's car is parked illegally. I was looking for her to ask her to move it. Barring finding her, I would have no choice but to have it towed; not a good way to ingratiate yourself with a local business owner. We have been meeting in this boardroom with your students regularly; asking you to wait for me here to discuss an agenda for Friday's meeting would be a plausible explanation."

I agreed, "Let's go with that."

Both Detectives Callahan and Barker responded to the call; they seemed taken aback to see the two of us once again sitting in the boardroom. Well, if we kept meeting like this, they would soon become our new best friends or worst enemies!

We had both skipped lunch, and someone's stomach was growling; much to my dismay, it was mine— how embarrassing. Food would have to wait; we were both about to be interrogated! Detective Callahan checked Sara for a pulse, making the same determination we had; Sara was dead.

Detective Callahan asked Trip if there was a room he and Trip could use for a confidential conversation?

"Yes, of course, we can talk in Meeting Room C, next door."

Detective Barker and I had the misfortune of staying put in Meeting Room D with Sara's dead body. "Someone had to be here to greet the medical examiner," Callahan advised.

Rather insensitive, I would think the norm would be to leave the guy with the body and take the female elsewhere. Silly me!

Once Trip and Callahan left, Detective Barker flatly said, "Start from the beginning; what were you doing in this room, Ms. McManus?"

"I was to meet Trip here for a planning session for my students' project. When I arrived, Trip wasn't here yet, and that is when I saw Sara slumped over the table."

Barker then asked me for a timeline, which I gave him. Following up with, "Did you know Sara, Ms. McManus?"

I told him I met Sara at a Rotary Club meeting two weeks ago and had visited her shop a week ago Friday. Depending on what else Detective Barker asked me, admittedly, my story could get a bit complex. Since Trip and I had discussed what we needed to tell the local police, at least our stories would be the same.

Omitting that Sara had not shown up at the March of Dimes Ball and that we spent the morning searching for her could cast suspicion on our motives for being here today! I am sure someone overheard Sara and Trip's conversation last Wednesday, witnessing her reaction to Trip's news, 'She wasn't his choice for the ball.' The fact that I was might also raise a few questions. I am sure people have killed or ended up dead over more minor issues. Sara's phone call to me would no doubt also come to the officer's attention at some point.

I really should put down those mystery novels for a while. Crime scenes and motives were coloring my life's perspectives. I digress. I tend to do that. As it worked out, our stories jibed, and the detectives seemed OK with us, for now.

Lucky for us, Sunday was not a very busy day, and there were not many employees working today. It still took the detectives several hours to question everyone. Detective Callahan told Trip to make arrangements with the employees who had worked Saturday night to come in early the following day. He would need to speak to all of them.

Crime scene tape once again blocked the entrance to the boardroom. I knew this could mean more lost revenue for Trip if meetings were scheduled there tomorrow. At 5 p.m., the medical examiner left, the employees whose shifts had previously ended sent home, and Trip and I were free to go.

The dinner shift was beginning when Trip and I entered the dining room. Selfishly, I was happy to see there were not many early diners, so much for my concern about lost revenue. At Trip's request, the hostess seated us at a table far away from other dinner patrons. We needed to talk, compare notes, and figure out what, if anything, we needed to do.

Trip noted, "I asked Detective Callahan if they had any new information about Hannah's murder?" To which Callahan raised an eyebrow, obviously meaning, "Not that I would tell you." To be expected, we were both on the wrong side of their investigation, maybe even possible suspects.

Trip told me that he had not disclosed Sara's absence from the ball, our looking for her, or Sara's call to my cell phone, the matters we agreed not to reveal willingly. I told him I hadn't divulged any of that either! Since they hadn't asked, we didn't feel we had done anything wrong. However, we could be *hauled* in for questioning once they found out. I couldn't help but mention, "They might also be disturbed to find out we have been bypassing them, looking into Hannah's murder ourselves. If they do find out, I will tell them it was my idea and not your fault."

"Not so, Maggie; I willingly became involved in trying to solve Hannah's murder; we are in this together."

Conversation lagged, and we both sat thinking about what we should do, if anything, about the death of these two women. This second incident would not bode well for the River Town Hotel and Conference Center. I was pretty sure my employer would not be happy to learn that, once again, my name and PSU would be in the news.

Our introspection was interrupted by our waiter. Tom greeted us, handing us a menu, filling our water glasses, and reciting that the evening special was Grilled Salmon, which included herbed rice pilaf and baby carrots. Tom asked, "Can I get you a beverage?" We both replied at the same time,

"Coffee." I told Trip the daily special sounded wonderful; no need to explore the menu. Trip agreed and placed our order.

Tom returned within seconds, carrying a tray with a basket of dinner rolls and butter, a pot of coffee, and a cream pitcher. Trip and I each selected a dinner roll from the basket and placed a pat of butter on our bread plates. Trip poured coffee for both of us, and I added cream and sweetener to mine. That first sip of coffee was heavenly—nothing like a "hot" ice breaker to cut through our introspection.

While waiting for dinner, we discussed the students' marketing project. Trip wanted to know if I thought we should proceed? I told him I needed to talk to my boss; I was hoping the university was open-minded and would let us carry on, but two deaths might cause concern that the students could be in harm's way. I asked him what he would like to do?

"I only want what is best for you and the students, Maggie."

I assured him I knew he did and offered, "Until we get to the bottom of these deaths, things are going to be complicated enough for you, Trip."

"Are you sure you want to continue looking into these deaths, Maggie?" "Well, if we don't, and they find out we were meddling in their investigation, we may become their number one suspects. Your thoughts, please?"

"I can't argue with any of that, Maggie." Dinner arrived; we both admitted we were starving and concentrated on eating our meal. Trip should take great pride in the quality of the food and service provided by his hotel. Dinner, as usual, was outstanding! The gentleman that he is, Trip, insisted on paying above my objection that we should at least split the check. I need to find a way to repay his generosity.

Trip drove me home immediately after dinner. I tried to keep the conversation light, steering away from the day's events by talking about the previous evening. I told him I liked Jennifer and hoped I would have the opportunity to spend time with her in the future.

Trip's response, "Easily done. Jennifer and Todd invited me to a party at their house next Saturday night. Would you like to go with me? Jennifer always tells me to bring someone, and you know my story about that. It is pot-luck, and everyone brings a dish to share."

I didn't need to think about my answer. Of course, I said, "Yes, I would love to go."

Trip told me he would call Jennifer and ask her what type of dish she would like us to bring.

"I will be happy to make whatever it may be. I love to cook, and I cook every chance I get, which isn't often enough."

Trip pulled up in front of my house. Turning off the engine, he got out of the car and opened my car door. Escorting me to the front door, he took my keys and unlocked the door for me. Planting a swift kiss on my cheek, he headed back to his car and drove away.

Now that I was alone, I was beginning to feel out of control; so much had happened recently; I needed to sit down and think things through.

Chapter Fifteen

I couldn't believe all that had transpired in just the past two days—I had to admit it wasn't all bad: I decided to recap everything; some of it could prove helpful later.

The March of Dimes Ball—Trip's confession about Sara, good food, good people, and dancing with the perfect partner were all at the top of my list. Sara not showing up at the ball, her phone message to me Saturday night—what was it she had to tell me that was so important?

Trip and I spent hours looking for Sara, only to find her dead in the boardroom. I dread my boss's reaction to my stumbling across another dead body at the hotel. Why did these two women end up dead in the same room at the hotel less than two weeks apart? Is there a connection? What was Sara's cause of death? Did Sara enter the hotel on Saturday night with anyone? How did she come to be in the boardroom? Who was drinking wine with her?

I still had lots of questions about Hannah's murder, as well. Had the knife that killed Hannah come from the kitchen? Was a funeral ever held for her? Had her parents planned or even attended it? If so, who else might have come to pay their respects? Did Sara attend or any of the men mentioned in the newspaper article? Who, if anyone, had collected Hannah's personal effects from her office? What became of those missing money and credit card fraud charges? Was anyone caught or convicted?

With all these questions floating around in my head, I couldn't imagine what was happening in Detective Callahan's and Barker's! They had probably collected much more information than Trip and I. It would be nice to pull these cases together and solve them!

I wanted to talk to Trip, not the detectives, about all of this. I suspected he had gone back to the hotel after dropping me off.

Tomorrow promised to be a hectic day for both of us. In addition to preparing for my two Monday classes, I would have to call Dr. Caruthers and Susan Crenshaw to tell them about Sara's death. Could it possibly be another murder?

I turned on the TV. The evening news might hold some answers. Surprisingly, Sara's death hadn't made the nine o'clock news, and I wasn't staying up any later. Determined to check the morning news, I set my alarm for 5:30 a.m. and got ready for bed.

I didn't feel rested or renewed when my alarm sounded. My Fitbit sleep tracker verified that I had spent more hours awake than asleep. Putting on my bathrobe and slippers, I went to the kitchen—first things first; I needed coffee.

I took my coffee to the dining room table and turned the TV to the local station, just in time to hear the 6 a.m. news anchor highlighting the stories they would be covering that morning. Sara Milligan's death was making the news today.

I sat and waited. The Anchor announced, "Now, let's turn to Trent Norris, who is covering a story at the River Town Hotel and Conference Center." Norris began by saying, "I am standing here in front of the River Town Hotel and Conference Center; a second woman has died here in less than two weeks. Sara Milligan, Owner of Dress for Success, was found dead here yesterday afternoon around 3 p.m. Police are investigating. We will have an update on that story later today."

Wow, neither Trip nor I received any mention. Guess Caruthers and Crenshaw might not be calling me this morning. I have a chance to place calls to them ahead of the new scandal.

Norris wasn't the only reporter there; I could see the news vans, camera operators, and reporters in the background, probably hanging out with hopes of interviewing Trip again. Two women found dead at the River Town Hotel and Conference Center within two weeks of each other was big news for a small community like River Town, FL.

The second cup of coffee helped with my sleep deprivation. I decided a bowl of oatmeal with brown sugar and two percent milk was the breakfast fortification needed to get me through this day. Sitting around sulking wouldn't help much. A Charles Swindoll quote, one of my mother's favorites, came to mind:

"The remarkable thing is I have a choice every day of what my attitude will be. I cannot change my past. I cannot change the actions of others. I cannot change the inevitable. The only thing I can change is attitude. Life is ten percent what happens to me and ninety percent how I react to it."

I entered my closet to work on my attitude; selecting clothes always affects my disposition. I thought a red suit, long sleeve white blouse with red piping around the collar, sleeves, and on either side of the buttons on the shirt's front was a cheery choice. Red pumps and pearl earrings completed today's ensemble; I was off to the shower.

Today is the last day of September. The university has been in session for five weeks. I spent several of those five weeks involved in two deaths. When the news finally breaks that I found the second body, my life might never be ordinary again, not that it was before I moved to River Town. Not quite the change I had envisioned for myself when I decided to change careers and leave Massachusetts.

Time to get those unpleasant phone calls out of the way. I picked up the living room phone at 9 a.m. and dialed Dr. Caruthers's office. She was in, and I unburdened myself, telling her I planned on calling Susan Crenshaw next. Dr. Caruthers's snarky response, "How do you manage to get involved in these very *imprudent* situations?"

I was taken aback and retorted, "Dr. Caruthers, I promise, I did not find the bodies of these women by choice; I was simply in the wrong place at the wrong time."

I took a deep breath and nervously continued, "Five of my Services Marketing students are working on a project at the River Town Hotel and Conference Center."

Before I could continue, Dr. Caruthers interrupted, chastising me, "I can't believe you allowed your students to become involved with *that hotel.*"

I immediately interjected, "I understand your concern; I am also concerned, but we are going into week six of the semester, and starting over with a new business would be a big disadvantage for these students. They are currently meeting with the general manager at the hotel for about an hour on Friday mornings. As the project evolves, they will need to spend four hours a week, at varying times, interviewing hotel guests."

Dr. Caruthers replied, "Under the circumstances, it would be ill-advised to have them continue with that hotel, find a different business for them to work with."

Thanking her for her time, I hung up.

To say I was upset would be an understatement; I was boiling mad! How could she blame the hotel or me for what happened to Hannah or Sara? Those two, I mused, must have been involved in something ill-considered that caused someone to want to harm them! But then, I realized how unfair that was. They were the victims. People are killed every day through no fault of their own. It certainly wasn't Trip's or my fault that this happened. I hated how Carruthers had emphasized *that hotel* as if it were the dregs of the earth? Was there something I did not know? Diana and Trip told me about the hotel's history; it had a reputation for poor customer service and inadequate upkeep. I would have to put that question on the list of things to ask Trip.

Susan Crenshaw was understanding, actually telling me she was sorry this happened to me. Once again, she cautioned me not to talk to anybody, especially reporters, about the situation saying, "Please have anyone from the media call me directly."

Gladly —same drill, different death; oh, dear Lord, why me? *Attitude,* I reminded myself, it will all work out.

I spent the rest of the morning preparing for my two afternoon classes. The Convention and Meeting Planning student's written field trip reports are due today. I was anxious to read them and plan on sharing some of them with Trip and Arlene. Today's class time will be devoted to their group projects, planning an event—groups will present ideas for their events to their classmates, seeking feedback and suggestions!

Groups in the Services Marketing Class will be reporting on the progress they have made in preparing blueprints with their community partners. An excellent opportunity for idea swapping.

I was ready for both classes, except for my new dilemma about terminating the River Town Hotel Project and finding a new organization willing to work with the students.

I needed/wanted to talk to Trip ASAP. I looked at my watch; it was 11:30 a.m. I decided to take a chance and call him. If he is unavailable because the police detectives are still there, I plan to leave a message with the front desk for him to call me this evening after 8 p.m.

With my mind made up, I dialed Trip's office. To my surprise, Trip answered promptly. I asked him if he had a few minutes to talk? I was relieved when he responded, "Yes, now is fine; Callahan and Barker just left."

Trip went on to share, "Last night, I contacted the employees who had worked Saturday night not already interviewed by Callahan and Barker. True to his word, Detective Callahan called me at 8 a.m. to tell me they were on their way over to the hotel. Detectives Callahan and Barker were surprised to see so many people waiting for them at 8:30 a.m. They spent the last three hours conducting what they called 'initial interviews.' Everyone understood that should more information be needed, there might be a second interview. So, for today, they are through here. However, journalists, TV news anchors, and camera operators have hung outside the hotel all morning. I have yet to talk to anyone. I needed a break and a chance to think about what to tell them."

I earnestly replied, "Trip, I would venture to say, as little as possible for now would be best."

To which he replied, "Affirmative."

I asked, "Have you had a chance to think about the marketing project?"

Trip replied, "No, actually, I haven't."

I hated to do this over the phone, but I told him what had transpired with Dr. Caruthers. "Well, I guess that decision is off the table, Maggie. She made it for us. What do you think her primary objection is?"

"I am not sure; she faulted me for involving my students with *that hotel.* Have you any idea why she would have a personal problem with The River Town Hotel and Conference Center?"

"None; I have never even met the woman," Trip replied.

"Maybe I am making more of this than I should."

Trip offered, "Or, she knows something we don't."

I told Trip about making a list of all the loose ends and questions about Hannah and Sara's deaths.

"I am going to do the same thing. How about we compare notes? I am super busy this week, but can you meet me at the Hotel on Friday at 10 a.m.?"

"Of course, ironically, you are already on my calendar for that day and time."

No sooner had I hung up with Trip, than my phone rang. It turned out to be Tim Swank calling to arrange a fundraising committee meeting. "So far, Wednesday at 10:30 a.m. looks good for most members."

"Great for me, wonderful use of time; our meeting will just roll right into the Rotary Club luncheon."

At last, I thought, a chance to ask him about those two men who had been harassing Hannah. I didn't want to ask him about this over the phone; there is something about facial expressions that speak volumes in addition to the spoken word; it would have to wait until Wednesday.

I arrived early for my 2 p.m. Convention and Meetings Class. No one uttered a word about the death at the River Town Hotel. I suspected that Trip was still awaiting interviews or a lag time in the reporting.

The five groups of students, much to my delight, had chosen five different types of events: a wedding, a comic con event, a charity fundraiser, a music fest for a local community, and a concert. These potential *future event planners* were eager to share their ideas for their projects with their classmates. This two-and-a-half-hour class flew by.

With only thirty minutes between classes, I usually stay in the classroom to prepare for the five o'clock class; today was no exception. Once students started arriving, I learned news had broken about the second death at the River Town Hotel. I listened to the students' versions of the local press reports. Of course, my name came up. One of the students told me a reporter had commented, "Finding two dead people was suspect; they would be following up on the story." Wow, an update planned on whether I had anything to do with the deaths. Trip had been interviewed and told the reporters he had nothing to report; he was waiting for the police to provide him with the cause of Ms. Milligan's death. Asked about Hannah Johnson's murder and if the two incidents were connected, Trip's noncommittal response, "The police are still investigating, and I have nothing to add."

It wasn't easy, but I finally got the students back on task. The element of detail and organization for all five blueprints led me to believe students were reading their textbooks. I said all five because I had made a last-minute decision to let the students working on the River Town Hotel Project share their plans. I did not tell them the project was off. I felt no need to drop the bomb until I could find them another community partner. No harm, no foul, I thought; I was pretty sure Dr. Caruthers might think otherwise.

Worn down and hungry when the class ended at 7:30 p.m., I stopped at Marco's Pizza on my way home. I ordered a cheese pizza and a garden salad made with a fresh-cut lettuce blend, cheddar cheese, black olives, onions, green peppers, sliced tomatoes, and croutons. I topped my salad with an oil and vinegar dressing. Looking around the restaurant, I realized there were not many people here this evening. I was able to get in and out in just over half an hour. I went to bed as soon as I got home, ignoring the flashing message-waiting light. I didn't even turn on the news. I would deal with all of this in the morning. I had had "enough day."

Chapter Sixteen

Tuesday morning: I was up at 5:30 a.m. I needed an early start to prepare for this week's online class. I continued to ignore the message-waiting light; coffee and breakfast first. As there was nowhere, I needed to be today; I could afford the luxury of hanging out at home in my pajamas and bathrobe. I would have plenty of time to take a walk later in the day. After a late dinner last evening, breakfast was plain Greek yogurt, and a toasted English muffin *lightly spread* with margarine and sugar-free strawberry preserves.

I fixed my second cup of coffee and sat down next to the dreaded telephone to listen to my messages. There were several messages from media outlets. I noted their numbers to pass along to Susan Crenshaw and promptly deleted them. There were a few hang-ups and an upbeat message from Jennifer, "Trip called and confirmed the two of you would be attending our pot-luck dinner on Saturday. Please make a dessert of your choosing for twelve."

The only other message was from Ann. "Hi, Maggie, I work at Dress for Success. Sara left an envelope in the office on Friday with your name on it marked "personal." Ann left her cell phone number, asking me to return her call.

I called Ann's number, relieved when she answered, and I wouldn't have to leave a message. I told her I was sorry about Sara's death and knew it must be a difficult time for her. I apologized for the delay in returning her call, explaining I work some evenings and didn't get home until late last night.

"I understand, Maggie, and yes, Sara's death was a shock for sure; I am still reeling over it! I just wanted to make sure that you got the envelope. I tucked it aside, I have no idea what is in it, but the police don't know about it."

I asked her where and when I could meet her to pick it up? She hesitantly replied, "I took the envelope from the store, and it is at my house."

Ann's hesitation indicated she understood she could be in trouble if the police found out she had been messing with possible evidence. She gave me her address saying, "I will be home all day." I thanked her profusely for being so thoughtful and told her I would come by at 1 p.m. to collect the envelope.

Well, well, well, whatever Sara wanted to tell me on the phone might have something to do with the contents of this envelope. I couldn't wait to find out what was in it; in the meantime, I needed to get my online class open and grade their quizzes. I finished working on my courses at 12:25 p.m. I dressed quickly in jeans, a pullover, and sneakers, entered Ann's address in my GPS, and drove over to her house. I parked my car in front of her house and started up the walk to the front door. Ann must have seen me coming; she opened the door before I could ring the bell. I introduced myself and once again thanked her for her thoughtfulness. She handed me the envelope. I got back in my car and headed home.

I will admit, I was concerned about what Sara had to say. Geared up for something negative, I opened the envelope. What she had to say was the opposite. Sara was embarrassed and humiliated that she had said awful things to Trip at last Wednesday's Rotary Club meeting. She liked Trip a lot and was disappointed that it had not worked out with him, but that was no excuse for her saying so many derogatory things about me.

Sara went on to say she was genuinely sorry for her jealous rant and asked me to accept her apology. She sincerely hoped we could both move past this and become friends. Sara concluded her heartfelt letter, "facing Trip would be difficult, but she also needed to apologize to him."

I wondered when she had intended to give me the letter. My address wasn't on the envelope, indicating she had not planned on mailing it. Perhaps this was something I might never learn.

I folded the letter and put it back in the envelope. It must have taken a lot for Sara to have written this. I undoubtedly would have accepted her apology if she had been alive, and I knew Trip would too.

So, what was Sara doing in the boardroom drinking wine the night of the ball? Had she decided she wasn't ready to face Trip and me once she got to the hotel? Someone must have interceded. In any event, Sara met with them in the boardroom instead of attending the ball.

Where had the bottle of wine come from; perhaps one of the hotel's bartenders had an answer. Why had she called me at 5:10 p.m.? Was she in the boardroom then? Coincidence or not that she and Hannah had both ended up dead in the Meeting Room D, the cursed boardroom?

My head was spinning. I needed to do something to take my mind off all this. Time to take that walk I put off this morning. I walked for over an hour. By the time I got back, it was after three. I was tired but emotionally in a better space.

Another lost lunch day. I opted for an early dinner and warmed up some leftover lasagna from the freezer, accompanied by romaine lettuce, tomato, cucumber, and a green pepper salad with a low-calorie Italian vinaigrette dressing. I turned the TV on and sat down at the dining room table to enjoy it.

I spent the evening watching the news and an *HGTV* show. There was no mention of Sara's death on the evening news.

Chapter Seventeen

Wednesday morning, I arrived at the River Town Hotel and Conference Center at 10:15 a.m., fifteen minutes early for the fundraising meeting. The reader board in the lobby included information about our session: Rotary Fundraising Committee Meeting: Meeting Room C 10:30 a.m. I walked down the hall and entered Meeting Room C. Tim Swank was already there and had set up the head table with agendas and other pertinent information for his new committee members. I approached him, asking, "Is there anything I can do to help?"

"Thanks for asking; I'm all done; we just need to wait for the rest of the members."

I told him I had thought a lot about what he had shared with me about Hannah's past and her problems with the boys from her childhood. I handed Tim the list Trip had given me. "Do you recognize anyone on the list?"

Tim studied the names before saying, "Albert Smith is the only name I recognize. The others may have been former students, but their names don't ring a bell."

Tim looked directly at me, ready to measure my response, saying, "Awful news about Sara. I understand she was found dead in the same room in the hotel as Hannah."

"Any ideas who may have disliked her enough to kill her, Tim?"

Tim hesitated before responding to my bombshell question, "Not really, but Sara was not popular in high school. Back then, rumor had it she had turned down an invitation to the prom; making matters worse, Sara had laughed at him. The consensus was Sara thought she was too good to associate with her classmates."

I thanked him for sharing his insight. Was a motive surfacing, perhaps an old grudge?

The committee members started to filter in, and I switched gears. I needed to concentrate on fundraising projects.

After half an hour of brainstorming, we came up with a list of ideas: car wash, spaghetti dinner, a holiday dance, selling raffle tickets for big-ticket items like a car or a cruise. Tim assigned each of us a fundraising idea to research. Lucky me, I got the cruise raffle. We left the meeting talking excitedly about our fundraising options. There is usually one person who throws a wet blanket on everything; I am happy to say there are no naysayers on this committee,

I was hungry and couldn't wait to taste whatever culinary delight the chef prepared for today's lunch. Entering the banquet room, I looked around for Trip; he was nowhere in sight, but there sure were lots of early birds. I wondered if they were here ahead of time to network or find out more about the hotel's second death. I ended up sitting with Superintendent Swank and members of the fundraising committee. We continued talking about our fundraising ideas until the meeting began.

All in all, it was an uneventful meeting. There was still no sign of Trip, when the luncheon ended. I know I could have asked for him at the front desk, but I reasoned he would have come to the meeting if he were free. But then perhaps Trip wasn't up for a grilling about the new death at his hotel by his fellow Rotarians. Disappointed, I walked swiftly to the parking lot and drove home. Patience is not one of my better virtues, but determination is. I wanted to know if Albert Smith was involved in Hannah's and Sara's deaths, and I needed to find that out.

I walked dejectedly into the house, dropping my coat and briefcase on the dining room table. I sat down on the sofa, twirling strands of my hair around my finger, a childhood habit I couldn't break. I thought long and hard about what Tim told me. There was no apparent tie between the credit card scandal and the deaths. What's next, I asked myself?

I spent the afternoon working with my online class and finished up just in time for the 6 p.m. news.

Turning on the local channel, I didn't have to wait long to hear the information I had been dreading. A local news anchor simply reported that Sara was dead and her body had been found at the River Town Hotel and Conference Center;

police were pursuing leads. Bummer, I wish they had at least disclosed the cause of death!

Thursday seemed to drag. Two students enrolled in my Thursday class are also part of the River Town Hotel project. I intentionally did not mention the canceled Friday meeting to them during class this afternoon. I was not ready to give anyone an explanation. They would have to read the email I intended to send when I got home.

I kept the message simple: "We will not be meeting at the hotel tomorrow—group members should arrange to work on the blueprint at the university tomorrow instead. I have every confidence the group can complete the blueprint without Mr. Evans and me."

I was anxious to meet with Trip tomorrow to see what he had to offer. I kept hoping the police would resolve Hannah's and Sara's deaths soon. I do not think law enforcement works any faster in real life than in novels.

Chapter Eighteen

T rip seemed just as glad to see me as I was to see him. It seemed like forever since we found Sara's body, was it only last Sunday! We had a lot to talk about this morning. The first thing I brought up was Tim recognizing Albert Smith's name, telling me Sara had turned down an invite to the prom and that her classmates did not like her.

Trip, taking this all in, sat thinking for a few minutes before responding, "I am not sure what to do about this. As a former employee, Albert would know his way around the hotel, and we now have learned that the superintendent of schools thought he had been harassing Hannah." Trip continued, speculating, "The police might have more information about the credit card fraud, and then again, it might have nothing to do with any of this."

I could only agree with him but added my two cents, saying, "I am still bothered by why the article was in Hannah's file? I believe there may be more to this story, but I am not sure how we can find that out. The only thing that comes to mind is to go back to the library and ask the librarian to help me look for additional articles. However, I think it unwise to call attention to ourselves."

I suddenly had an inspiration, "Trip, do you suppose your friend, Clara, would be willing to research this for us? As a former librarian, this would be right up her alley."

"Great idea, Maggie; I am certainly willing to ask her."

I changed gears asking, "Have you heard anything about the knife?"

"Yes, Callahan finally told me on Monday that the stab wounds indicated the knife had a narrow-serrated blade. I asked the Chef, but he wasn't sure it was necessarily a kitchen knife. He said he would ask his staff if one of their kitchen knives fit that description. Any other questions come to mind?"

"Yes, quite a few; my mind has been racing lately! Do you know if anyone at the front desk saw Sara enter the hotel, and did she come in with anyone? Was the bottle of wine a type sold by the hotel, and had anyone bought a bottle that evening?"

"Intuitive questions and I don't have the answers. The police detectives questioned everyone on duty that night and should know."

"But Trip, they are not about to share that information with us! Do you think it would be OK to ask your staff?" I knew he was carefully weighing his answer; there could be consequences if the detectives thought he was interfering in the investigation!

Finally, he replied, "I can't see why that would hurt."

I added to Trip's list of things to do, which made me feel terrible! But far worse was allowing this investigation to drag on with no end in sight! Taking on Hannah's duties, I was sure Trip was already over the top.

I cringed, remembering there was still one more thing we needed to address. "Did anyone pick up Hannah's belongings from her office?"

"Yes, actually, her mother came by to get them. She was torn up about Hannah's death, blaming herself for not staying in closer contact with her. She admitted to their having differences and confessed she should have called her and not let anything interfere with their relationship, sobbing, 'Now, it is too late.'"

"Do you know what their issues were?"

"No, I don't—I wish I had asked her, but with her daughter dead, it didn't seem like the right time to pry into their failed relationship."

"Trip, there is a time and place for everything; that certainly was not the time to pursue their failed relationship."

"My concern," Trip replied, "is that perhaps there may be some underlying reason for the rift attributable to Hannah's death."

"That is possible—was there anything in Hannah's belonging that might offer any clues?" Trip thought for a minute and replied, "Only her daily planner; her mother wouldn't need that, and the detectives didn't ask for it."

I shook my head, saying, "Unbelievable—why the heck not. They should have!"

Trip offered, "We could start by looking at who she was meeting with that day or had been seeing regularly. I looked at the planner but only from the standpoint of contacting people with whom Hannah had made appointments."

Trip excused himself and went next door to Hannah's old office, bringing back her planner.

Unfortunately, after carefully reviewing it, nothing seemed to hold any significance. Hannah had made appointments that month with many different people representing companies wanting to book meetings and events. None seemed personal or too repetitive. For the moment, we were both out of ideas, and Trip had to get back to work. He walked me out to the lobby asking, "Are we still on for Jennifer's party tomorrow?"

"Yes, of course, I am looking forward to it!" He swung the front door of the hotel open for me to exit.

I knew Trip was watching me walk to my car. He has developed a fixation with my trendy outfits and usually makes clever, quirky comments about my attire. I had fully expected him to mention my red, yellow, and green print scarf artfully tied around my neck, being reticent of a set of traffic lights. But he didn't. It was hard to have a light and airy conversation or focus on anything other than the two murders these days.

The lackadaisical investigation conducted by the detectives was a serious matter and left us no choice but to take matters into our own hands! Ironically when I returned home, I found Detectives Callahan and Barker parked in their patrol car in front of my house, lying in wait for me. I pulled into my driveway, and they got out of their car and followed me to the front door. Callahan told me he had questions about Hannah's and Sara's deaths and asked if it was OK for them to come inside? What could I say? Unlocking the front door, they followed me in. I placed my briefcase on the dining room table and offered them a seat on one of the sofas in the living area.

Settling myself on the couch across from them before asking, "What do you need to know?" Barker was the one who spoke, saying, "Ms. McManus, how well did you know Sara Milligan?"

"I told you last Sunday that I didn't know her well at all." I sensed that Barker was unhappy with my curt reply and added, "I sat with her during a Rotary club meeting and bought a dress for the March of Dimes Ball from her store."

"Who did you attend the ball with," Barker asked?

I hesitated slightly before saying, "Trip Evans."

"Did you know that Mr. Evans and Ms. Milligan were dating?"

"Trip told me about that the night of the ball. What has that got to do with her death," I asked? Callahan scowling at me, chimed in, "Were you aware that Trip and Sara had harsh words the Wednesday before her death?"

"Yes," I cautiously replied, "I learned about that also the night of the ball."

Without batting an eye, Callahan asked, "Were you jealous of their relationship, Maggie?"

"What relationship, Trip told me they had one date, and they attended two Chamber of Commerce Meetings together. For gosh sakes, that would not constitute a relationship in my mind, and that was months ago, long before I arrived in River Town.

"Besides," I countered, "My friendship with Trip is, founded on business interests that have nothing to do with Sara."

Smirking, Barker asked, "Why did you go to the ball with him, then?"

"Trip invited me because he had an extra ticket and didn't know anyone else to ask. He also told me since I was new in town, that would be a good way to meet people. I agreed to go, and that was all there was to it."

"You have been spending a lot of time over at the hotel since Hannah's death," Callahan remarked.

"Yes, I have. The River Town Hotel hosts the Rotary Club, of which I am a member. I attend meetings every Wednesday. Trip is, or was, working with a group of my students on a marketing project. The students and I had been meeting with Trip on Fridays until my boss, Dr. Caruthers, told me that, because of the two deaths at the hotel, that was not advisable."

Callahan and Barker sat studying their notes. I decided to bring this interview to an end, saying, "Anything else that needs clarifying, detectives?"

Callahan looked up at me, but before he could respond, I looked him in the eye and said, "I guess you haven't made any progress finding the killer, or you wouldn't be grabbing at straws. I had no motive to kill either of these women. The timing is off; I can't be in two places at one time, now can I? I was touring the hotel with Trip and my students when Hannah was killed and attending the ball with Trip in plain sight of lots of people all evening the night Sara died."

Realizing his blunder in trying to establish a motive for me when I had alibis for the time of both deaths, he became docile, "Sorry, Ms. McManus, we are just trying to rule out all possibilities."

I decided to use this to my advantage and boldly asked, "Detective Callahan, what was Sara's cause of death?" He replied, "Sara's wine glass contained a poisonous substance."

"Were the contents of the bottle poisoned as well?" Callahan never hesitated, responding, "No, the bottle was fine."

I asked about the time of death and, once again, was given a direct answer. "I can't be sure, Ms. McManus, but the ME thinks around 9 p.m."

Guessing he had decided to trust me, I pressed on. "Does anyone know where that bottle came from?"

"Yes, Ms. McManus, the wine is one that the hotel stocks … which outlet we have yet to learn." "One more question, officer. What time did Sara get to the hotel, and did she come in alone?" "That's two, Ms. McManus, and you are pushing it," was his cranky reply before he continued. "The receptionist remembers her entering the lobby before 6 p.m. alone to the best of her recollection."

The detectives stood up at the same time, and Callahan said, "We need to be on our way. Thank you for your cooperation and time. If you can think of anything that might help with the investigation, please let us know."

I ushered them to the door.

Wow, I got answers to some of my questions; having them show up trying to blame me, as scary as it was, actually worked to our advantage. Perhaps I should forewarn Trip, but there was no need we had alibis for both murders, and they knew that. Trip and I were both off the hook. The puzzling piece is why Hannah and Sara were murdered at the same hotel and in the same room two weeks apart? Murder, Sara was murdered! She certainly wouldn't poison herself while drinking wine with someone else, would she?

Chapter Nineteen

S aturday morning, I was up early drinking coffee and wondering what dessert to make for Jennifer's potluck dinner. I finally decided on a universal favorite, cheesecake; my mom's recipe with cherry topping always receives rave reviews. I had planned a food shopping trip to Publix this morning; I added the ingredients I needed to the shopping list. Cheesecake needs time to refrigerate; I had better shop early. I tacked on a few more errands to my morning outing: gas up the Camaro, run it through the car wash, and a stop at the dry cleaners.

I hate letting a day get away from me when I have so much to do. I was off to run my errands by 8 a.m and home by 10 a.m. Time to make the cheesecake.

I decided to wear comfortable, casual attire to the party— black, brown, and white leopard print palazzo pants with a black turtle neck sweater and gold hoop earrings. Perhaps a little dramatic, but a fun, spirit-lifting choice.

Trip was ringing my doorbell at 5 p.m. sharp; a punctual male and a GM no less. Kudos to Trip. I often ran late when I was a GM. The hotel, so far, must be quiet on a Saturday evening. I opened the door for Trip, and I knew I had chosen wisely. The man laughed, saying, "You never cease to amaze me."

I grinned at him, eyeing his attire, tan khakis, and a red plaid shirt; "Red is definitely your color!"

I retrieved the cheesecake from the fridge, put it and the cherry topping in food carriers, and we departed for Jennifer's house.

Jennifer and Todd Davis live in a sprawling ranch situated on several acres on the outskirts of River Town. As we drove up, I noticed several outbuildings to the rear of the house; one I learned later was a barn where they stabled a few horses; Todd was a former equestrian medal winner and gave riding lessons on the weekends. Jennifer's and Todd's three children and their spouses were already there. Bart and Glenda Flanagan arrived right after us—making up our pot luck party of twelve.

Small towns have their good and bad points; everyone always knows everyone else, creating a real sense of community. However, that said, no one is ever safe from scrutiny over possible conflicts of interest or gossip. Later in the evening, I learned that Bart was not only the attorney for the River Town Hotel and Conference Center but handled closings for the Davis real estate business. He had also handled Sara Milligan's legal transactions. Small town, small world.

Jennifer introduced me to her family members and other guests, adding offbeat, trivial tidbits about each person. She laughingly said, "Maggie is the woman who can't stop finding dead bodies in Trip's boardroom."

It turned out I didn't get to spend much time with Jennifer, after all. She was pretty busy making drinks, warming up food, and clearing tables. I envied Jennifer's relationship with her children and their spouses. With my parents both gone, I was alone, an orphan—no siblings, dotting grandparents, aunts, uncles, or cousins. However, there is something to be said for creating your own family from close friends and associates. I was very grateful that Jennifer's family warmly welcomed me into their inner circle this evening.

I love potluck dinners. You never know what tasty eats to expect. Tonight's feast was an eclectic assortment of delicious foods, starting with Glenda and Bart Flanagan's specialty, a Mexican seven-layer bean dip served with Tostitos Chips.

Jennifer's main course was an Italian dish—Chicken Marsala; Chicken breasts sautéed, then braised in Marsala wine and cream with mushrooms and green onions.

With Jennifer in charge, it was one of the most organized potlucks I had ever attended! Jennifer had assigned Cybil and her husband, Shawn, scalloped potatoes, a family favorite from the Davis family recipe collection, to accompany the Chicken Marsala.

Jennifer's daughter-in-law, Jessica Davis, married to their eldest son, Jeremy, was assigned to salad duty. Jessica made a—romaine lettuce, dried cranberries, mandarin oranges, and toasted walnuts—paired with a cranberry-orange vinaigrette.

Davis's family members, Lillian and her husband, Jim, are into bread making, and Jennifer asked them to make her favorite crescent rolls, always a big hit.

I love baking and was happy to have been assigned dessert! I proudly admit my cheesecake with a cherry topping was also a huge success.

Jennifer had asked Trip to bring several bottles of wine. I am not sure Trip knew or remembered this, but one of the bottles of wine was the same kind Sara had been drinking when she died. I can't seem to get away from those death thoughts!

"All had a good time" is an understatement. I felt like I had known these people my entire life. We exchanged lots of laughter and *stories*, leading me to share what I learned about Sara Milligan. I know, I said, that I hate gossip, but this is different; any clues we get about the victims, the better our chances of finding the killer(s).

Naturally, with the death of Sara fresh in all of our minds, the subject was bound to come up. Bart told us that, as Sara's attorney, he had been worried about her for some time. She was having financial difficulties, and he had contacted a local banker who helped her consolidate her loans.

It sounds like Sara might have been living beyond her means. I didn't say this to anyone, but she had expensive tastes; the car she drove her home in an upscale neighborhood, the diamond jewelry she wore, and of course, her clothes were top of the line. I had no idea how much revenue an upscale boutique could generate in a small town like River Town.

Bart told us he was in the process of probating her will. I wondered who would inherit her business and decided to rephrase the question by coming in through the back door asking, "Is the store to remain open?"

"Unfortunately, no, Maggie," Bart said. "After Sara's will goes through the probate court, then the new owner decides what to do with her assets, which includes both her home and business." Trip followed up, asking, "What about Sara's employees?"

Bart offered, "They will be able to collect unemployment until they can find new jobs."

The tricky question, who inherited, was broached by Jennifer. After all, the business and home could end up for sale. It would undoubtedly benefit Jennifer and Todd's real estate business to obtain both listings.

Bart prefaced his answer, "Sara asked me to draw up her will just last month. She was very concerned about who to name as her beneficiary. Sara's parents are deceased; she has one sibling, an older sister, in central Florida. There was a family dispute over inheritance, and the two sisters have not spoken since her parents' death."

"Sadly," Bart said, "Sara told me she didn't have any close friends; acquaintances, yes. Willing her estate to someone was a real dilemma. She finally decided on her sister, Susan."

Bart seemed annoyed, and I wasn't wrong. He continued by saying, "It's not my job to pass judgment, but sometimes I don't agree with my clients. Sara instructed me to send Susan a copy of her will and a letter telling her she was the beneficiary of Sara's estate. It seemed almost surreal to be calling her weeks later about her sister's death. Susan told me she was taken off guard, never expecting to hear from her sister again. Sara had made it clear she wanted nothing to do with her.

"Susan begrudgingly agreed to honor her sister's wishes for no formal funeral service and made the arrangements for Sara's interment next to her parents at the local River Town Cemetery. She announced her death in the local paper, mentioning her burial place and nothing else."

After Bart recounted Sara's final arrangements, the room was utterly silent.

I couldn't help myself; finally breaking the silence, I said, "What a sad ending to a life. Who could have hated her enough to kill her?"

No one responded— Sara's death was becoming more mysterious by the minute.

The party broke up at about 10 p.m., early for a Saturday night in some circles. I was glad I was in this one. I rarely stay up later than 10 p.m. I collected my cheesecake carriers, and Trip retrieved my jacket. We walked out to the car, waving goodbye to Jennifer and Todd, who remained standing in the doorway watching their guests depart. I realized that Trip, and I had not had much time to talk to each other this evening. We had spent much of the evening acclimating me to the other guests, answering questions from Jennifer's family members about how Trip and I had met.

I could hear Trip relating the tale of my teaching at PSU and bringing my class to the hotel for a field trip and working with him on a school project.

I had pretty much relayed the same story with no mention of there being anything personal between us, and yet attending a friend's party together might be construed as a date. I had no idea how Trip viewed this and was almost afraid to ask. Given his staunch denial that his last two outings with Sara were business events—leaving me with the unanswered question, because she asked him to attend, or because they were Chamber of Commerce events?

I was running this through my mind when Trip spoke, "Maggie, I had a wonderful time tonight. Thanks for coming with me. Since I moved to River Town, Jennifer and Todd have become my best friends. I was delighted that you hit it off with Jennifer at the ball. I could tell that their children liked you and accepted you into their close-knit family circle this evening."

I smiled and hugged myself in the darkness of the car, saying, "I love Jennifer's and Todd's family; they made me feel so welcome. I am grateful that you asked me to come with you, Trip."

I needed to talk about Sara and said, "I feel bad for Sara; it is a pity that her relationship with her sister took such a wrong turn. Why would she not want a funeral service so that people could pay tribute to her and say their goodbyes?"

Trip quietly responded, "Maggie, Sara admitted to Bart, she didn't have any close friends; maybe she felt no one would come anyway, so why bother?"

I solemnly responded, "I sure hope that doesn't happen to me."

"Not a chance. You and Sara have entirely different personalities. People seem to take to you right away like the 'Davis Clan' did this evening."

Humbled by his kind words, I simply replied, "Thank you, Trip."

We were both quiet after that, caught up in our thoughts about the evening. Trip parked his car in my driveway and walked me to my front door. I thought about asking him in, but as I wasn't sure about our status this evening, I thought it might be presumptuous to offer him coffee or a nightcap. So, I didn't.

Trip took my keys, but before he opened the front door, he bent down and kissed me gently on the lips. I admit I had been hoping that would happen. I could feel my heart racing and swear I heard the "bells and whistles" I read about in romance novels.

I responded warmly to his kiss; he put his arms around me and kissed me again, but this time with a more prolonged deeper kiss that found me responding with a longing that had been building for some time. He gently released me from his embrace and opened the door, saying, "Goodnight, Maggie, I will call you tomorrow. We need to talk."

A simple "Goodnight, Trip" was all I could muster; I went inside and closed the door.

It was late, and I went into the bedroom to get ready for bed. But I couldn't stop thinking about what had just transpired. What did "We have to talk mean?"—admitting to myself that I knew very little about Trip, and for that matter, he doesn't know much about me either. Right now, we are working on pure chemistry and "in like" with each other. I do know that I want to spend as much time as possible with Trip, and it won't matter doing what.

Chapter Twenty

Trip sounded tired when he called me at 9:30 the next morning, and I asked, "How did you sleep last night?"

"Maggie, I lay awake most of the night. My sleeplessness brought on thinking about Sara and Hannah's deaths, your students, and I admit thoughts of missing you. I was up early contemplating what you and I or the local police can do to move the investigation along.

"The revelation that Sara's estranged sister inherits the Dress for Success boutique and Sara's home may have nothing to do with her murder and probably, disgusting thought, *a dead-end.* Things that appear irrelevant might have some bearing on the case; *every stone needs to be unturned to get to the truth and find justice for these women.* Where did that come from!"

Laughing, I said out loud, "Trip, try, Superman. 'Truth, Justice, and the American way.'"

"I sure don't feel like Superman, just a frustrated GM."

Trip was in a talkative mood and continued by changing the subject, "I need to say something about last night; I found you attractive on the first day I met you. Kissing you was long overdue. I don't know where this will lead, but I am willing to open my heart and see what happens."

"I thoroughly enjoyed you kissing me," was my heartfelt response! "Which is one of the reasons I couldn't sleep last night either. I kept reliving the moment."

I loved Trip's response, "Well, we will have to try it again soon."

I would love to have said, when? But instead replied, "I would like that a lot, Trip, can't wait."

Begrudgingly, it was now my turn to change the subject, "Trip, I need to tell you about my visit from Callahan and Barker; they tried to make the case that I was jealous of your relationship with Sara and had a motive to kill her. I told the detectives we were only business acquaintances."

"Maggie, we have nothing to worry about, even though we have begun dating."

"We have?!" I exclaimed.

Trip kiddingly said, "Gee, Maggie, when I invited you to Jennifer's and Todd's party, should I have asked, would you like to go out on a *real date* with me?"

"Very funny, Trip, and yes, you should have. I didn't know our relationship had changed in your mind; I only knew what I would like to happen in mine."

"Now that we are on the same page, Maggie, I hope we will have lots of other *real dates.* Laughing, I replied, "I hope so too, Trip."

I changed the subject again, soberly, saying, "Trip, there is more I need to tell you about my home visit from Detectives Barker and Callahan. I was able to get them to admit that the ME classified Sara's death as murder by poison. Her glass contained the poison, but not the bottle. Sara's approximate time of death is recorded as 9 p.m. Saturday. Witnesses verified Sara's arrival at the hotel on Saturday was around 6 p.m."

˙ "Well, that visit was revealing; at least they seem to be doing some investigating! I still have no confidence in those detectives' ability to locate Hannah and Sara's killers. Look at the things we found out that they never even considered. To have peace of mind, I think we need to continue looking for clues to ferret out the killers ourselves or insist the police do their job. The hotel's reputation is at stake, and I am worried it might affect my job. I have kept the hotel owners up to date, but they are concerned. These murders are hanging over the hotel like a tornado about to be unleashed."

Thinking about the cause of death, I asked, "Trip, can you find out what hotel outlet the bottle of wine Sara was drinking came from and who bought it? Also, as the police detectives told me, the receptionist stated Sara arrived before 6 p.m. Saturday, and alone, it would be helpful to know the exact time and who saw her enter the hotel, and if anyone followed her in?"

"Good point; I am planning on viewing the tapes from the hotel's security cameras for that night. Hopefully, the footage will disclose some helpful information. Can you come over to the hotel and view them with me today? Two pairs of eyes will certainly be better than one."

"Of course. I can't believe there are tapes of the entrance; this could be a game-changer!"

Trip's attitude shifted once again when he confided, "Maggie, I am concerned about the quality of the police investigations. I came up with that idea on my own. The detectives haven't even asked me if the hotel has surveillance cameras."

In an attempt to lighten up, he said, "I must have gotten that idea from those crime shows I love to watch on TV."

"You're kidding, Trip; I love watching crime shows; *Castle*, *Bones*, and *Criminal Minds* are my favorites."

"Well, we will have to watch some of those shows together. I don't suppose you read mystery novels?"

"Yes, I love mysteries. Connolly is my favorite; I love his *Lincoln Lawyer* and *Harry Bosh* series."

We had been on the phone for at least half an hour, and I was sure Trip had things he needed to do. I agreed to meet him at the hotel at 1:30 p.m. and hung up.

Chapter Twenty-One

I didn't have anything earth-shaking to do before heading to the hotel to meet Trip. It might be helpful to add to my notes about the two murders. Sara's death, now classified as a murder, took place between 6 p.m. and 9 p.m., depending on how long the poison took to kill her. Tying down the exact time she drank the wine may not be possible. But at least we now had a smaller window of time and knew the wine came from Trip's hotel. Hopefully, today, Trip will be able to find out exactly where and who might have purchased it.

According to Trip, Hannah's mother had collected her belongings and was still grieving Hannah's death. We also learned that Tim Swank thought one of the Hotel's former employees, Albert Smith, had been harassing Hannah and maybe Sara.

I was hoping that Trip would enlist Clara's help in finding out more about the missing money and credit cards. We needed to either verify this or remove it from our list. Then, I had almost forgotten—why hadn't the security guard found Sara's body in the boardroom? Security guards have to keep written records of their rounds; where were the ones from Saturday night? Another question for Trip.

This whole investigation is getting out of hand. I am constantly worrying that we are missing something important. Even writing things down leaves me feeling scattered. How can we possibly keep it all straight in our minds? How do criminal investigators do this every day for a living?

I reread my previous notes looking for anything that I might have missed that would lead me to the killers! Nothing popped off the pages. I closed the file and prepared to head over to the hotel.

The front desk receptionist told me Trip was waiting for me in the boardroom. Visiting the boardroom was becoming scary; as pretty as this room is, I always dread what I will find on the other side of the door.

I cautiously pulled the door open to find Trip sitting at the table with a pile of bar checks in front of him. Suddenly, I felt shy and didn't know what to say or do. Trip spotted me and quickly came to my rescue. He got up from his desk, closed the boardroom door, and reached out for me; encircling me in his arms, he whispered in my ear; it is so good to see you, and then he planted a soft kiss on my lips and let me go.

"Back on task," he said, "I have been going through the bar checks from Saturday to see if I can determine the source of that wine bottle. I have isolated the bar checks containing that type of wine. I am now looking to see what time they sold and who purchased them. Only seven bar checks include the sale of this wine. I helped him scrutinize each of the checks. Most

143

names were unfamiliar and appeared to have been ordered by hotel guests having dinner in the dining room. But one bar check indicated Sara Milligan had purchased a bottle at the service bar at 5:45 p.m. using a credit card. With that revelation, we were even more confused. Trip and I packed up the bar checks and brought them to his office for safekeeping. He made a copy of the check showing Sara's signature, placing the original, the duplicate, and the others in a desk draw and locking it.

Trip glanced at his watch. "The daytime security guard should have left by now. Let's go to the security office and review the tapes from the night Sara died—the new security camera system is state-of-the-art technology but is easy to use."

We found the footage from that Saturday and began examining the activity at the front door starting at 5:30 p.m. As we continued to watch the monitor, we saw Sara arrive by herself at 5:40 p.m. She stood in the lobby for a minute as if she were trying to decide where to go. Bingo, she headed in the direction of the bar.

We continued to watch the tapes. We were hoping to see someone following Sara into the hotel. No one went in the direction of the bar for the next ten minutes. Sara was next seen at 5:55 p.m. by herself with two empty glasses and an open bottle of wine heading past the front desk in the direction of the boardroom corridor. We continued watching to see if anyone was following her. From 6 p.m. onward, people attending the ball entered the hotel lobby through the double doors in large numbers. We scrutinized each segment several times to identify the people we knew and segregate the ones we didn't. Or I should say Trip did. Most of these people were new to me, faces may be familiar, but I had no names to attach to them. I was one of the 6 p.m. arrivals.

"Wow, Trip, I missed seeing Sara by minutes."

Speculating out loud, Trip said, "Who knew she had gone to the boardroom? Why two glasses? Sara obviously expected someone to meet her there!"

Sighing, I added, "Why do all these leads always pose even more questions?"

Trip and I were both deeply disappointed. We hoped the videos would contain clues about who might have killed her. We sat thinking for a while, and then I broke the silence, "Trip, do you have the footage from the day of Hannah's murder?"

"Yes, I do, Maggie. Sara's and Hannah's deaths were only two weeks apart and in the same month and should be easy to find." Trip found the correct tape and began scrolling through the footage for the right time frame.

Suddenly I remembered I hadn't told him about Sara's letter to me. I gave Trip a summary, stating, "Sara was sorry about her treatment of you, Trip, and what she implied about me. She hoped we could all be friends."

Trip stopped scrolling, looking at me, his face registering shock and then relief. "Did I hear you say Sara was feeling remorseful about our confrontation at the Rotary luncheon the day before the ball?"

"Yes, that was the essence of the letter."

"Thanks for telling me, Maggie; I feel better knowing that Sara didn't die hating me."

Trip spoke out loud what I, too, had been thinking. "I can't get past the fact that Sara came to the hotel dressed to attend the ball. I wonder what made her change her mind; why would she buy wine and take it to the boardroom to drink? She could have just consumed it at the service bar where she bought it."

I chimed in, "But Trip, don't forget what her lawyer told us; she didn't have any real friends, and facing us together may have been more than she could endure."

"Well, that may be true, Maggie, but confirming her attendance the day before the ball and then meeting someone before the ball tells me she was moving past that."

"I think we are getting a little closer to finding out what happened to her, Trip. Her phone records would show if she called anyone once she got to the hotel. For what reason would anyone need to go into the boardroom after 5:55 p.m., unless they knew she would be there or saw her go in?"

Trip wasn't quite so sure, "Closer? We have no way to access her phone records, and at some point, soon, we need to share what we know with the police detectives. They can access phone records, know who worked that night, and have already talked to everyone who was there."

"True, perhaps we are spinning our wheels, and they have already uncovered someone with a motive."

Trip and I decided to follow Hannah's video trail another day. It could take hours to review those tapes; we were both exhausted. It was almost four o'clock, but. I couldn't leave until I asked, "Trip did you read the security guard's report for the night of Sara's death?"

"Yes, I looked it over," was Trip's welcome news.

"Surprisingly enough, there was no mention of anything being out of order that evening. The guard had ticked off the rooms on his checklist as if he had gone into them. I doubt he checked these rooms or anything else. And Maggie, the same security guard, had been on duty from 9 p.m. Saturday until 5 a.m. Sunday. I am going to call Callahan tomorrow to find out what they know about this guard and his trumped-up report."

I rose to go. Trip followed me to the front door and walked me out to my car. He unlocked the door for me, saying, "I will call you tomorrow."

I reminded him I taught classes most of the day and wouldn't be home until 8 p.m.

"Well, I guess I will just have to be patient and wait till Tuesday to talk to you."

A quick kiss on the lips and we parted company, left with our thoughts of what we had just uncovered. Me, well, I was also thinking it would be nice to spend time cultivating a romantic relationship!

Chapter Twenty-Two

Trip's Point of View

Trip sat in his office for a long time after Maggie left. His evolving relationship with Maggie made him smile. However, Maggie's revelation about Sara wanting to apologize to him made him feel small. He had belittled her, telling her he didn't consider all of the times they went out actual dates. That must have been embarrassing for her. If anyone was due an apology, Sara was, and now it was too late.

Knowing she had bypassed the ball and bought a bottle of wine to take to the boardroom made him feel even worse. How the poison had gotten into her glass was puzzling. Did she know it contained poison? The unthinkable, did she kill herself? If so, what was going through her mind while she was drinking? Who sat across from her drinking only half a glass? Was that person the killer or an enabler? So much to think about, way too much.

Trip thought about staying to view the footage of the day Hannah had died. He decided he didn't have the heart to do it today, especially not alone.

He did not want to go home and chastised himself for not asking Maggie to have dinner with him. Maggie left just half an hour ago. How could you miss someone in just half an hour!

Trip's thoughts turned to his beautifully restored colonial house only a few streets from the hotel. When he bought the house, he had planned on walking to work. He had yet to do that. Since he started this job, he had spent almost every waking hour working. Today, he had the chance to leave early and felt like there was no reason to go home; he hated being alone. He was not sure why he felt that way. He had lived alone most of his working life, except for the brief time he had been married to Sissy.

Over the years, he had often thought about getting a cat but viewed it selfish to leave an animal alone for hours and hours at a time. Perhaps he could walk home for lunch every day and spend some time with the cat. He could use the exercise, and it would be a way to take his mind off work for a while.

Maybe Jennifer knew someone with a cat or perhaps a kitten in need of a kind owner with a comfortable home. This thought perked him up, and he picked up the phone and dialed Jennifer's number.

Jennifer was breathless when she answered the phone. Trip asked her if she was alright?

She replied, "A little out of breath. I just finished feeding the horses. I heard the phone ringing as I approached the house and ran to get it."

Trip thanked Jennifer for her hospitality the night before, telling her he would reciprocate for all those times he had spent at her house; my housewarming party is way overdue.

Jennifer, true to form, enthusiastically replied, "Trip, what a great idea. I would be happy to help you put one together."

"Thanks, but not necessary, Jennifer. I have a catering staff at the hotel that would be happy to earn extra money and show off their skills. For once, you and Todd could be guests and enjoy the evening."

Trip then broached the subject of acquiring a cat. Surprisingly enough, Jennifer responded, "Does Maggie have any allergies to animals?"

He didn't know and told her so. Jennifer's response said it all. "Well, if you are planning on spending time with her, asking her would be the right thing to do."

Did Jennifer mean asking her, as in, to get married? Of course not; she was referring to allergies. I wondered what was in my subliminal mind that jumped from cat allergies to marriage. In any event, the fact that we like each other must be evident to Jennifer and probably everyone else who has seen us together.

I had zoned out and realized Jennifer was talking to me!

"One of our barn cats had a litter of kittens, and you are welcome to bring Maggie out to look at them. I highly recommend you adopt two. When you are busy, they will keep each other company."

"Jennifer, I love your methodical approach to cat adoption. 'Mother to the world,' you are!" I told Jennifer if I found out that Maggie was OK with cats, I would ask her to help me pick them out. Would next Friday be OK?"

"Of course. Friday evening would be a good time for me to get to know Maggie better, and I will order Pizza."

"No," Trip said, "I will bring the pizza. I will call and let you know what Maggie says."

Jennifer agreed to my getting the pizza, saying, "Don't bother calling, come over with or without Maggie, and whether you are looking for cats or not. See you at about 6 p.m." She hung up.

I decided not to wait until next Tuesday to make plans with Maggie for another "Davis' outing." I picked up the phone and dialed Maggie's number.

Maggie was home and delighted to hear from me. I told her about Jennifer's invite for Friday. She enthusiastically told me she was free and would love to go.

I couldn't imagine Maggie not being fond of animals, but some people, as much as they like them, are allergic and can't be around them. She must have thought I had gone daft when I changed the subject to pets, asking her if she had allergies to cats or dogs?

She replied, "I am not allergic, and I love dogs, but cats hold a special place in my heart. They are so independent and self-sufficient to boot, but they are your best friend for life when they bond with you."

That clinched it. I told Maggie about my plan to pick out two kittens from the Davis' litter of barn cats Friday night.

"Why two?"

"That was Jennifer's idea; she convinced me that since I am not home much, they will keep each other company."

"Oh my gosh, Trip, maybe I could get one too. I am home a lot, and one would work!"

I had a visual of Maggie excitedly jumping up and down on her couch. I started laughing, and then Maggie began laughing. It felt so good to be feeling lighthearted and joyous; I hadn't felt that way in a very long time. I had a positive outlook before my divorce from Sissy and the rift with my parents. Thinking about them just ruined the moment for me. Why did I have to go there? I told Maggie I had to go, collected my car keys from my desk drawer, and left the office for home.

Chapter Twenty-Three

C offee in hand, I sat down at the dining room table. We are now entering week seven of the semester, and my procrastination has left me with the same dilemma I had last Monday; what to do about the River Town hotel project. Last Thursday, instead of telling the group I needed to find them a new project, I sent group members an email telling them we would not be meeting at the hotel to work on their blueprint at the university.

Then, in a flash, I had a revelation. The students and I did not need to meet at the hotel to complete the blueprint. Neither Trip nor I needed to be present for the students to isolate the contact points between the customers and employees. They had enough knowledge already to determine this on their own. Last Monday's class had focused on each group's plan for organizing their blueprints; the River Town Hotel Group had already demonstrated their ability to complete the design by themselves. If they had any questions, I could follow up with Trip for them.

The project's next phase requires students to interview guests about their interaction with hotel employees. Students could use questionnaires and surveys to fulfill that part of the project. Not as good as personal contact, but at least the students could continue with their hotel project. After Dr. Caruthers's comments, my allowing them to continue was risky. Once the murderer(s) are caught, Dr. Caruthers will have no reason to insist I find another project. I will check with Trip tomorrow and gamble he will go along with my plan.

Relieved that I had a solution, I turned my attention to reviewing my lesson plans for today's classes. The Services Marketing class will be focusing on the textbook chapters about Understanding Customer Expectations and Building Customer Relationships. The Convention and Meeting students will use class time to coordinate their event plans; it should be an exciting class.

After all this worrying and planning, I needed a walk to relieve my stress. The temperature in the Panhandle of Florida has been gradually declining. I put on long black and gray gym pants and a matching long sleeve shirt. It felt good to be out in the fresh air, breathing clean air into my lungs. After my exuberating walk, I felt much better, regaining confidence that everything would work out just like it was supposed to.

I was starving and devoured a bowl of cornflakes with two percent milk and another cup of coffee. In high spirits, I began looking through my closet for the perfect fall outfit. I don't mind cold weather; it's fun to get creative around the seasons. I was smiling from ear to ear when I spotted a scarf delicately embroidered with yellow and orange flowers and found an orange turtle neck sweater to match.

I still had plenty of time before my two o'clock class. I grabbed my murder file and sat down on the couch to review my notes. I was hoping to find something that I may have overlooked, anything out of the ordinary that might provide clues to the motives for the murders. I still thought their deaths were related somehow and wished I could put my finger on what that might be.

These women may not have traveled in the same circle as adults, but they attended the same high school as teenagers, and both probably attended PSU. If Superintendent Swank was correct, the boys who harassed them in high school were still harassing them all these years later. One of whom, I was pretty sure, was Albert Smith.

Albert was one of the men included in the newspaper article found in Hannah's personnel file. Albert had worked at the River Town Hotel for a short time; he would know his way around the hotel and have known Hannah.

According to Sara, Hannah was at a local bar recently with two men who had been giving her grief. Sara had also indicated these men might be the guys Hannah had hung out with when she was in high school, almost too coincidental. What did Albert know about the two deaths, and how could we find that out?

I sure wish I knew more about Albert Smith and his relationship with these two women. The detectives must have him on their radar. He is probably one of the two men carted off to the police station—way too much speculation.

Chapter Twenty-Four

Tim Swank called me on Tuesday to tell me the fundraising committee would not be meeting on Wednesday morning. The members needed more time to research their fundraisers. I realized I had forgotten about looking into a cruise fundraiser. That was very irresponsible of me, but I was relieved I wasn't the only one who needed more time; I decided to dedicate the rest of the day to conducting research. I could not risk forgetting again. I need to be ready for next Wednesday's meeting.

Trip called me shortly after I hung up with Tim Swank. I listened attentively as he updated me about his conversation with Callahan. "I told Callahan I suspected the security guard hadn't inspected anything that night and that I didn't think the previous owners had bothered to conduct background checks on anyone, even security guards with huge responsibilities.

"Detective Callahan confirmed I was right about both things; Roger Barrett, the security guard in question, had an arrest record, dating back many years, for auto theft. When Callahan cornered Barrett about the hotel and Sara's murder, he admitted he had not inspected the hotel that night, sighting being busy because of the March of Dimes Ball.

"I asked Callahan if anything else had turned up during his questioning of Barrett?" Callahan's harsh response, 'NO!' So typical of Callahan's communication style, he hung up without saying goodbye.

"Well, it looks like I need to replace this useless security guard ASAP. One more thing off our murder list; however, one more thing on my GM list."

"Maggie, before I forget, I was able to connect with Clara. She agreed to look for follow-up articles on the newspaper story from Hannah's personnel file."

"That is a big relief. If there is anything to learn, Clara will uncover it!"

Weighing heavy on my mind was my concern that someone needed to speak to Albert Smith, and soon! I shared that with Trip. He agreed, saying, "Once we find out what Clara uncovers, we can decide what to do next."

I told Trip about my plan to have the students work on their hotel project at the university instead of the hotel.

"Brilliant idea, Maggie."

I am relieved that you are willing to go along with this, Trip. If the students have any questions, I can be the go-between and contact you."

Trip ended the call saying, "Looking forward to seeing you at the Rotary luncheon tomorrow."

I sat thinking about all the loose ends Trip had tied up surrounding both cases. Hopefully, we will have a chance to talk more after tomorrow's luncheon.

I arrived at the Rotary Club meeting fifteen minutes ahead of time. I love these meetings; the food is delicious, and the members I have met so far are all upbeat, interesting people.

I was planning on networking, hoping to meet new people, but Trip, standing with Mayor Scott, Attorney Bart Flanagan, and Banker Harold Thorpe, spotted me and pointed to an empty table. We all headed for the table, and I sat down next to Trip. Todd Davis quickly filled in the remaining seat, causing me to chuckle, "hail, hail, the gang's all here." Trip's friends greeted me warmly, expressing their delight in seeing me again so soon.

So much for networking and meeting new people; this suited me just fine. The meeting started promptly at noon, and so did the first course. I leaned over, getting Trip's attention, saying, "Oh, my goodness, this is the best baked salmon I have ever had. The dill mustard sauce and the spinach salad are a perfect accompaniment." Dessert was a large slice of German chocolate cake, beautifully presented on a plate decorated with crème-colored icing and garnished with berries.

The meeting was uneventful, except for the president's announcement that the fundraising committee was still diligently working on ideas. I was glad I had done my research and could contribute something next week.

Our table mates stood up and quickly left the room as soon as the meeting ended. Trip's first remark once we were alone, "Are you trying to give the Grinch who stole Christmas a run for his money?" Today I was wearing a lime green dress with a full skirt and long sleeves, trimmed with double rows of white rickrack around the neck and along the bottom of the dress. I had paired it with a broad white patent leather belt, sparkly lime green earrings, and a matching bracelet. I had even unearthed lime green high-heel pumps.

I laughed and cheerfully responded, "No, I am missing a red Santa hat," sparking Trip's laughter, followed by a silly grin.

"Are you still planning on picking out a kitten on Friday, or have you reconsidered? Pets are a lot of work, you know."

Cautiously I replied, "While I was growing up, my mother and I always had a cat. We both loved them. Our last cat was named Skunk. He was a beautiful black and white; we were devastated when he died of old age; he was eighteen. I had forgotten how much I missed Skunk's company until you mentioned Jennifer's barn cats. Skunk was technically mom's cat, but Mom and I were very close; we spent a lot of time together."

I knew this revelation could spark questions, which is why I usually provide limited information about myself.

Trip asked, "Did you and your mother live together, then?"

It dawned on me I was revealing things that were painful to revisit. But I ventured on, "Yes, after Mom retired, she moved in with me."

There must have been something in my demeanor that changed because Trip just reached over and hugged me and did not ask any more questions. We agreed he would pick me up at 5:30 p.m. on Friday. He would place an order for Pizza, and we could pick it up on the way to Jennifer's and Todd's house.

Ah, the life of the working set. Trip needed to get back to work, and so did I. This afternoon, I had work to do with my online class. Trip told me he would call me as soon as Clara got back to him, expressing confidence that Clara would turn up information to help us move forward. Clara will also talk to Jennifer to see what she has to say.

I hated to go home; it was a beautiful fall day, and I would love to be outside, but duty calls. I crossed the parking lot and got into my Camaro.

Reliving my conversation with Trip about my mother and Skunk, I was surprised that mentioning my mother hadn't sent me into a meltdown like it usually does. My counselors' words still resonate today, "People handle the grieving process in different ways; one thing is for sure, though, the grieving process takes its own sweet time."

Trip had quickly discerned he needed to drop the subject of my mother, ironically just as Jennifer had. How fortunate was I to have such caring, intuitive friends!

Friday morning— Adoption Day! I decided to search for my cat carrier and litter box, just in case I brought a kitten home tonight. I found them on a shelf in the garage and carried them inside the house. I washed the carrier and placed a small plush throw in the bottom. I didn't think Trip would have a pet carrier, but if he decided to adopt, I was pretty sure Jennifer would have one he could borrow. I made a spur-of-the-moment run to the store for groceries; cat supplies were on the top of the list. I picked up enough litter for Trip and me and a litter pan for Trip.

I was waiting on the porch with the cat carrier when Trip arrived at 5:30 p.m.

Just because I was wearing jeans and a bright pink novelty shirt depicting cats of varying breeds and colors, accessorized with a pair of dangly cat earrings, was no reason for him to laugh quite as long and loud as he did. Oh well, far be it for me to begrudge anyone a good laugh.

I handed him the cat carrier, he put it in the trunk, opened the passenger door for me, dropped a kiss on my lips, and closed the door. He walked around the car, got in on the driver's side, turning to look at me; he started laughing all over again. My wardrobe always brings out the humor in him. Watching him laugh, I couldn't help myself—laughter is contagious—I started laughing with him. Wiping the tears from his eyes, Trip started the engine, and we headed downtown to pick up the pizzas from Marco's. I was looking forward to the evening, and I knew Trip was too.

Todd spotted us as soon as we arrived and came out to help Trip carry in the pizza and beer. Jennifer and I had spent a few evenings together, but always in the company of other people, leaving us little time to get to know each other. I knew from the few conversations we had that we would become friends.

Jennifer stands five feet four inches tall and matches me freckle for freckle. Her mid-length dark brown hair is beginning to gray, and she openly says she doesn't plan to color it. Jennifer's expressive chocolate-brown eyes are usually covered with her signature large-rimmed, bright red glasses.

Greeting me with a big hug, Jennifer handed me some napkins to set on the kitchen table. We followed up with plates, glasses, and silverware.

The four of us cozied up to the kitchen table, and Jennifer opened the pizza boxes. After drinking a few beers and eating several slices of pizza each, we were in good spirits. Jennifer suggested we look in on the barn cats while it was still light out. I couldn't wait to see them, and we followed Jennifer out to the barn.

Todd led the way to the back of the barn. Jennifer crouched down next to four tiny kittens curled up together on a blanket placed on top of a pile of hay. Jennifer's thoughtfulness encompasses animals and people, another reason to admire her.

To be expected, the mother cat was a little wary of us at first, but Jennifer patiently stroked her multi-colored fur until she calmed down. "Our timing was uncanny," Jennifer remarked, "the kittens are twelve weeks old, an age the Vet says is old enough to be separated from their mother."

I asked Jennifer if I could pick them up. Jennifer nodded her approval. I reached out to the mother cat first. She let me stroke her, and after a few minutes, I reached over and began stroking the kittens one at a time as the mamma cat looked on. Trip followed suit, petting each kitten and then carefully examining it. I asked Jennifer if there was a kitten she preferred to keep for herself?

"Not really," was her unselfish reply, telling Trip and me to decide which ones we would like to adopt. I asked Trip if he had any preferences?

"I love them all; you choose first."

I picked up a gray and white female. I held her close to my heart and stroked her; she commenced to purr. Love at first sight for both of us.

Jennifer had no problem with our taking the kittens home that night, and just as I suspected, she told Trip she had a cat carrier he could borrow. I told him I had picked up a litter box and litter for him, and all he would need was some cat food. Jennifer interceded, saying the kittens were partial to a particular brand; it would make sense to keep them on it for a while. She went back to the house to get cat food and a cat carrier while Trip retrieved my cat carrier from the car.

Trip picked up two squirming kittens and placed them in Jennifer's pet carrier while I situated the little gray and white in mine.

Smiling from ear to ear, he said, "I can't believe we are adopting kittens from the same litter." Our pizza night was turning out to be a short evening. We needed to get the kittens set up in their new homes.

Trip and Todd carried the pet taxis to the car and placed them on the back seat with the kittens facing each other, hopefully having a quieting effect on them during the ride to my house. I set the two cat food boxes on the floor in the rear of the car and got in. Trip started the engine; the kittens not to be silenced mewed loudly all the way there.

Trip hoisted my cat carrier from the car, and I retrieved a cat food box and opened the front door to let him in. He set the cat carrier down on the living room floor, gathered me into his arms, kissing me softly; he whispered, "Thanks for another lovely evening, Maggie, I will call you tomorrow." Picking up the cat litter and litter box by the front door, Trip walked down the porch steps toward his car; I watched him drive away.

My new kitten was still mewing loudly, wanting out of the pet taxi. I opened the door, and the curious little thing set off to explore. It was only 8:15 p.m., and kitty and I had plenty of bonding time left this evening. While she was roaming around, I filled her cat food dish and placed it and a bowl of water in an out-of-the-way corner in the kitchen. I had already put her litter pan in the spare bathroom earlier in the day.

I turned the TV on and waited for her to return to the living room. I sat thinking about what to call her. Instinctively, I knew I would name her Lily after my mother. As it turned out, Lily did not come back to the living room. I found her sound asleep curled up on the afghan at the foot of my bed. I turned off the TV and got ready for bed, sliding under the covers trying not to disturb Lily.

I discovered Lily is an early riser; she began to stir at 4:30 a.m. Guess I know who will be dictating our sleep patterns. She walked around my head a few times and then jumped off the bed. It was a pretty high jump, but that didn't seem to bother her. I got up, put on my bathrobe and slippers, and went to the kitchen to make a cup of coffee. Lily, the clever little thing, had already found her corner and was happily eating her food. I couldn't wait to hear how Trip made out with his two kittens.

Saturday morning, there is no place I have to be today. Pleased that I had gotten the grocery shopping out of the way yesterday, I made a second cup of coffee and went into the living room to catch the early morning news. It wasn't long before Lily joined me on the couch; gently petting her, she settled down next to me; thoroughly enjoying the attention, Lily commenced purring.

As I stroked Lily, my mind wandered to last evening, suddenly realizing that Jennifer hadn't mentioned talking to Clara about the murder victims or the men in the newspaper article. Perhaps they hadn't connected yet. Hopefully, Clara will call Trip today about Jennifer's take on these people and her research.

Long about 7:30 a.m., I decided to get dressed, eat breakfast, and start my housecleaning chores. Not wanting to leave Lily alone, I deferred my morning walk. I would see what the day brings and perhaps take a nice long walk later in the day.

Pardon the play on words; Trip called at 9:30 a.m. with, *Tails of his two kittens*. He told me he had decided to call them Harry and Sally after his favorite movie *When Harry Met Sally*. What a romantic! Harry and Sally had spent the night curled up together in a chair in his living room. At some point between last night and early this morning, they had eaten most of the food he had put out for them. They were eager to follow him around the house when he got up at 6:30 and spent the morning chasing each other around the house. They must have worn themselves out; they are now back in the chair, napping.

I told him about naming my kitten Lily after my mother. He replied, "Maggie, Lily is a beautiful name. I am sure your mother is smiling, heartily approving."

We spent time bragging about how smart and loving our kittens were, echoing the same sentiment, "We were glad we had decided to adopt."

Our conversation inevitably turned to the murders. I asked Trip if Clara had called yet.

"Yes, this morning. Clara told me that she had finally connected with Jennifer late last night. She apologized for calling me so early but couldn't wait to tell me what she had found out.

"While she couldn't find anything more about the credit card fraud and theft, it so seems that, according to Jennifer, contrary to what Superintendent Swank had told me, Albert Smith and Hannah had begun dating while they were in high school. They had even run away together; her parents had called the police. When the police caught up with them,

Hannah's parents had forbidden her to see Albert ever again. Hannah, however, continued to see him behind their backs, causing a permanent rift with her family when they found out.

"Clara also told me that Jennifer heard Hannah and Albert had recently broken up, creating quite a stir at a local bar. The police showed up, taking Albert and the man with him to jail. Hannah was allowed to go home but refused to press charges. Albert's police records verify this story. Could this breakup possibly be a motive for Albert killing Hannah?"

Odd that Tim Swank thought Albert had been harassing both Hannah and Sara. Dating was a far cry from harassing. Trip and I were stumped; we didn't know what to do next. The police detectives would undoubtedly have connected the dots between Hannah and Albert themselves. Then there was Sara. What motive would Albert have to kill her? It's hard to believe it was a coincidence that they were murdered in the same room two weeks apart?

Finally, I offered, "Trip, probably nothing we can do about Albert, but we still have a few loose ends to tie up. We could look at the hotel tapes for the day Hannah died. Maybe someone will show up on the hotel tapes around the time of her murder. Also, have you had a chance to talk to the bartender to see who else was in the bar the night of Sara's death?"

Trip said he hadn't spoken to the bartender yet and would do that today. Hesitating, trying to decide what to say next, Trip finally asked, "Would you be willing to come to the hotel Sunday afternoon to look at the tapes for the day of Hannah's murder?"

"Yes, I would be happy to help." We arranged to meet at 1:00 p.m. and hung up. The rest of the day was uneventful. I stayed home and followed Lily around.

Chapter Twenty-Five

When I arrived at the hotel on Sunday, the front desk receptionist told me Trip was waiting for me in his office. Trip's office door was open, but he wasn't there. I walked in and wandered around, waiting for him to return. I couldn't help but notice the photo on his desk, which appeared to be of Trip, and his parents. The picture made me realize I didn't know much about Trip's family or personal life. That was also true for Trip and my situation. At some point, we need to have a get-acquainted discussion.

When he finally arrived, he found me looking at his parents' picture, saying, "That is a story I will share with you someday soon. How long have you been standing there?"

I shrugged, "Maybe a half hour or so."

He laughed and said, "No way."

"OK," I admitted, "only a minute or two."

Leaving Trip's office, we went to the security office to begin viewing the tapes. While he was setting up the recordings, I asked, "Did you learn anything from the bartender?"

"Bad luck; the bartender is off this weekend. He won't be on duty again until Tuesday evening."

"Well, that is a shame; I am running out of patience, which never was one of my better virtues anyway," I confessed!

We began reviewing the footage of the front door and front desk area for the day of Hannah's murder, starting at 8 a.m. Trip noted every person who was in or passing through the lobby. None seemed to be out of place. Some people dressed in business attire were probably attending the session in Meeting Room B. I asked Trip if he knew the name of the group?

"Yes, I do. It was a local group of twenty attendees called "Young Professionals." Some of the young professionals looked familiar. One person we both knew was Sara.

"What did Sara's presence in the hotel that day mean, if anything, Trip? Was she there to attend the meeting of Young Professionals?"

"I don't know, Maggie, but I can easily find out by calling the meeting planner for the group first thing Monday morning."

We continued watching the tapes, which turned up a flurry of activity when the students started arriving. We fast-forwarded through the footage up until 11 a.m. that day. No one else stood out. We admitted we hoped Albert Smith would be on tape, but as we had no idea what he looked like, we couldn't be sure if he had been there or not.

"During his employment, Albert would have used the employee entrance," Trip said. "But Albert would have been

Marcia Dove

long gone before I installed the security system, which required employees to pass background checks to obtain access cards. Albert could no longer enter the hotel without an access card via the employee entrance." Just in case, we added checking the surveillance footage from the cameras located at the back entrance for the days of both murders to our list of things to do.

After finishing viewing the tapes from the front entrance the morning of Hannah's murder, we went back over the videos of the front door and lobby the night Sara died. No one seemed out of place. It was getting late, and I told Trip I needed to go home.

"We covered a great deal today, Maggie. We can view the footage of the back entrance another day."

Ever the gentleman, Trip walked me to my car, took my key, unlocked and opened the car door for me, but not before bending down and kissing me goodbye. Unlike the previous Sunday, Trip and I both had responsibilities at home; Harry, Sally, and Lily might need human companionship, but if not, at very least someone to replenish their food and water dishes.

Monday morning Lily, once again, had me up early. However, I was grateful for the 4:30 a.m. start; I have a ton of work ahead of me to prepare for today's classes. I hadn't spent any time working on them over the weekend, and now I am in crunch time. I plan on having the marketing students work on creating customer service questionnaires. Their questions will pertain to customer satisfaction for all the contact points on their blueprints. Once they have finished the questionnaires, students will be ready to meet with guests.

The students in the convention and meeting class will be using this week's class time to work on group projects. Their event planning project outlines are due next week. I have reminded students on more than one occasion that meeting planning takes a tremendous amount of coordination; the devil is in the details.

Late morning my thoughts were interrupted by the ringing telephone. I picked up the phone to hear Trip's voice excitedly say, "Maggie, Sara was at the Young Professionals' meeting, but she left early, 10:15 a.m. to be exact."

I couldn't help almost shrieking, "You're kidding; that is too coincidental. Sara may have had the opportunity, but what possible motive could she have for killing Hannah?"

"I have no clue; this is all very bizarre."

I interjected, "From what Jennifer told Clara already, I suspect Jennifer can help us tie the relationships between Albert, Hannah, and Sara together in a more meaningful way. I will be attending the Chamber of Commerce Networking Lunch with Jennifer this Friday. I will try to find time before or after the meeting to ask her."

"That's a great idea, Maggie."

I sensed Trip had moved on and was focusing on something else. His silence was a dead giveaway; I waited quietly for him to continue. When Trip finally spoke, he began, "I am not sure how to broach the subject of the murders and our relationship, Maggie; both are weighing heavily on my mind.

I decided that the best plan is to say what I am thinking and let the cards fall where they may!

"I am starting to feel overwhelmed; I desperately want the murder investigations to be over, and the killer(s) caught. The murders are taking up most of our free time. Time we should be using to enhance our social life."

Trip paused again, seemingly thinking something through. I waited with bated breath for him to continue.

"Maggie, I would love nothing more than for us to move on and commence a relationship free of mystery and intrigue. I think we owe it to ourselves to spend some time alone getting to know each other better."

I listened intently, my heart in my throat as Trip continued bearing his soul!

"Undoubtedly, we will see each other at the Rotary Club meetings on Wednesdays and continue working on your student project. But I must confess that's not enough. I don't want to make a habit of entertaining you solely at the hotel either; we need a reprieve from both jobs. I want to take you out on a formal date. Someplace where we can enjoy each other's company, have a nice meal, and ideally even dance. Are you free Saturday evening?"

His heart-rendering revelation touched me. My own heart still pounding, I responded, "I agree, Trip. I, too, am anxious for the murders to be behind us. Working on our relationship should be our main focus, and yes, I am free on Saturday evening and would love to go out on a formal date with you."

I could sense Trip's relief and knew he was smiling as he replied, "I am looking forward to Saturday, Maggie. I will pick you up at 6 p.m." Before hanging up, he laughingly added, "Now I can get back to work."

Chapter Twenty-Six

M onday's classes went well; I was thrilled that the students in both courses had become immersed in their projects. The time flew by, and the last class was over before I knew it. I didn't want to stop at a local restaurant for dinner on my way home like I usually do. I was tired; after all, I had been up since 4:30 a.m. I also didn't want to leave Lily alone any longer today.

Heating up lasagna from the freezer, I sat quietly eating and thinking about Trip baring his soul this morning. I was glad he had been brave enough to vocalize what I, too, had been feeling. The impact of his words on my emotions today was exhausting. An early bedtime was definitely in order.

Tuesday morning, I woke up with a start! I lay in bed thinking about the loose ends regarding Hannah's and Sara's deaths. We need to find a way to wrap the murder investigations up; the sooner, the better! We have narrowed things down considerably. Left to do: viewing the tapes for the employee entrance for both days of the murders, talking to the bartender to get a clearer picture of who was in the bar the night Sara died, and finding out more about Hannah and Sara's relationship with Albert Smith from Jennifer and Tim. Hopefully, something would come of this, and we would know who the killer was. Trip was right; we need to become more focused on our jobs and personal lives.

Since tomorrow will be another full day, attending Tim Swank's fundraising committee, followed by the Rotary Club luncheon and working with my online course, I plan on chilling out today. I don't have anywhere to go this morning. I plan to hang out in my pajamas and pay some attention to Lily. My walk can wait till later in the day. I turned on the TV to catch the news. It dawned on me that nothing had been reported about the murders lately. Was that a good thing or bad? I decided to go with; no news is good news.

Wednesday, I arrived fifteen minutes early for Tim Swank's fundraising committee meeting. I planned to ask him about the relationship between Hannah and Sara. Unfortunately, several other committee members were already there, and the opportunity did not present itself. Hopefully, I can corner him before or after the Rotary Club meeting. It appeared everyone on the committee had been busy with their fundraising assignments. As it turned out, the committee unanimously decided to commit to the cruise fundraiser. The cruise promised to reap the most significant monetary returns for the least effort I was now in charge of the Rotary Club's primary scholarship fundraiser for the year. I told the members that the cruise fundraiser primarily involves motivating club members to sell raffle tickets. I would have the tickets printed and distribute them to Rotary Club members as soon as they were ready. The committee meeting ran a little late, and everyone, including Tim, hurried off to the luncheon. Well, perhaps I will be able to talk to Tim after lunch.

I spotted Trip sitting with Mayor Scott and Bank Manager Harold Thorpe. Trip pulled out the chair next to him, and I joined them; much to my delight, sliding in next to me was Tim Swank. Smiling up at Tim, I asked, "Can you stay for a few minutes after the meeting? I want to ask you a question about Sara and Hannah." Tim admitted he was actually in a hurry to get back to the office, but if I had something that needed a quick answer, that would be fine.

"Tim, I promise to be quick!"

Tim took out his phone to check his messages. Sitting quietly, I couldn't help overhearing Trip's conversation with Mayor Scott. The mayor asked him if he was interested in serving on the committee to explore the relocation of the County Court House? Trip had accepted, saying, "Anything that enhances the community affects our hotel, and I would love to be a part of that." Mayor Scott interjected, "I will be calling a meeting in the next few weeks to begin looking into locations."

"Looking forward to the call," Trip replied.

The president called the meeting to order. Following the pledge and grace, the wait staff got busy serving the fare for the day: Baked flounder, grilled asparagus, and baked potato with a choice of condiments—butter, sour cream, bacon bits, and cheddar cheese. Dessert was a strawberry shortcake made with fresh strawberries, homemade biscuits, and whipped cream.

I was lost in thought about the hotel as I ate; The River Town Hotel and Conference Center always did their best to create *memorable meals*, a marketing tactic that was sure to pay off.

Who wouldn't want to book their functions here after experiencing the excellent service and delicious food? The answer— someone afraid of getting murdered, two murders were bad for business!

With the wait staff quietly clearing the tables, the president resumed the meeting; no visitors or new members today, and he forged on asking for committee chair reports. Tim Swank reported the news about our cruise fundraiser, saying, "A big thank you to the committee members for their expeditious work on selecting a fundraiser. A special thank you to Maggie McManus, who has agreed to take charge of the cruise raffle ticket arrangements." The cruise news received a round of applause. The secretary and treasurer read their reports, and the meeting adjourned on time.

Trip and my table mates, except for Tim, rose and departed as soon as the meeting adjourned. I looked over at Tim and quickly posed my question about the relationship between Hannah and Sara.

His response was informative but entirely unexpected. His brief statement, "I think Sara was jealous of Hannah; even though Sara was always perfectly dressed and had better grades than Hannah, Sara was a loner and didn't seem to click with the other students. Hannah was popular with the boys and had several girlfriends. Sara, pretty much, just kept to herself."

I thanked him for his time, and he left.

Looking around for Trip, I saw him standing at the entrance to the meeting room, waiting to hear what I had learned from Tim. I joined him, and we walked back to his office. Trip closed the door, pulled me close to him, and gently kissed me, whispering, "I've missed you."

He is such an affectionate man. "You have a way of always making me feel special," I said.

"That's because you are," Trip replied.

I blushed and said, "Thank you."

We sat down at our usual table in the corner of the office. Trip began by saying, "I have some good news to share with you, Maggie. I found a replacement for the security guard I recently dismissed and hired a marketing director to replace Hannah. With a new marketing director in place, we can finish the hotel's long overdue marketing plan."

"Thank goodness, Trip, with all you have going on, it must be a huge relief to fill those key positions."

"That it is, Maggie, that it is."

"So, what did you learn from Tim?" My reply was almost verbatim to what Tim told me, "He thought Sara was jealous of Hannah. Sara was a loner and didn't seem to click with other students. Hannah was popular with the boys and had girlfriends as well. Sara pretty much just kept to herself."

Neither of us knew what to make of this. If anything, we would have thought it was the other way around. We couldn't wait to hear what Jennifer's take on their relationship was and how Albert factored in.

Trip said, "Well, aren't you going to ask me who else was at the bar the night of Sara's murder?"

"Of course, I am. Was there anyone there that night?"

Trip smirked, saying, "You are not going to believe this; Mark, the bartender, admitted Albert was there. Coincidentally, Mark was one of the employees mentioned in the credit card article, the only employee who still works here, and the one I talked to right after finding the newspaper clipping in Hannah's file. Mark never mentioned Albert during that interview, even though his name is also included in the article.

"Tuesday evening, when I spoke to Mark, he informed me that he and Albert had been friends since high school. I had no idea there may still be a connection between Mark and Albert since Albert no longer worked at the hotel. I never thought to ask Clara the name of the other man who was with Albert the night that Hannah and Albert broke up."

"Trip, could it have been Mark?"

Trip continued, "Possibly, but to confuse things, Mark told me Albert was there before Sara arrived. Also, according to Mark, Albert never said a word to Sara, not even a perfunctory 'hi,' when she showed up. Albert departed right after Sara left the bar."

"Interesting," I said, "this means Albert was in the hotel and had the opportunity to murder Sara. What reason would he have to kill her? We could recheck the tapes to see if a man left the bar around the time Sara did. Unfortunately, we don't know what he looks like." Trip replied, "Maggie, there are way too many dots to connect, and Albert's presence at the bar opens the situation up to more speculation."

Other than talking to Jennifer about her take on these relationships, viewing the tapes from the employees' entrance around the time frame of both murders, I don't know what else we can do."

"Trip, was there anyone else in the bar besides Albert?"

"Yes, Mark said no one notable, though. He told me a few people who were finishing pre-event cocktails left about the same time Sara did." Once again, Trip reiterated how overwhelming this was becoming.

"Frankly, I have to agree; I am praying for closure!"

I rose to go, and Trip followed me to the hotel's front door. Before Trip could open the door, looking up at him, I asked, "By the way, have you decided where we are going Saturday night?" Trip gleefully replied, "I hope you like surprises, Ms. McManus, because you will have to wait until Saturday to find out; formal dining, and I will pick you up at 5 p.m. instead of 6 if that is OK?"

"I love surprises, and 5 p.m. is fine." Trip opened the door, and I walked quickly toward my car. I unlocked the door, slid in, and sat thinking about our dinner date. I do love surprises;

I have had too few good ones in my life. Trip's effort to create mystery around our date was touching and amusing. Smiling, I had to admit that Trip was genuinely growing on me.

An early Friday morning walk and breakfast out of the way, I sat drinking a second cup of coffee and thinking about my lunch meeting at Hooligans with Jennifer. I was looking forward to spending time with her and meeting chamber members. The sun was shining, but the temperature dictated I would need a jacket of sorts. My navy-blue pinstripe wool suit with a white blouse would be perfect, and wearing my PSU name tag will make introductions easier for the people I meet today.

I sat for a while thinking about Trip; I wonder if he will resume attending the Chamber of Commerce meetings now that he no longer needs to avoid Sara? Funny how we always overlook topics like this when we talk. I decided I would not bring up the murders during our dinner date on Saturday. Instead, I will ask Trip about his family and what growing up as an only child was like for him.

I had no idea if he had ever been married or had children. We had never really talked about ourselves, except when I mentioned both my parents had died. That conversation had quickly moved on, and although I had been grateful he didn't push for more information, I knew I couldn't shut that door forever.

Saturday may very well test our growing relationship; how much was either of us willing to divulge? Were we destined to keep secrets that would ultimately destroy our chance of an intimate relationship, one that I felt pretty sure we both wanted?

Jennifer was waiting for me at the front door of the restaurant when I arrived. We got in line, paid for our lunch, and bought 50–50 raffle tickets. Jennifer and I found a table for four, and as soon as we set our pocketbooks down to reserve our seats, people began gravitating toward us. Jennifer is well-known, and before the meeting started, she introduced me to quite a few people. It turned out that our two table mates owned a local retail store. Jennifer kept the conversation flowing through lunch, asking about their shop and changes to their inventory.

Lunch was superb; Hooligans prides itself on home-style cooking, meatloaf, pot roast, and chicken pot pie, the latter of which happened to be today's offering. I am always up for comfort foods, and chicken pot pie is one of my favorites.

The meeting format, I quickly learned, begins with new members, like me, introducing themselves and promoting their businesses. After which, all members have an opportunity for a two-minute infomercial to promote theirs. When it was my turn to speak, I stood up and cheerfully announced, "My name is Maggie McManus; I am a hospitality instructor at PSU and always in need of local businesses willing to work with my students on group projects. During the spring semester, students will be preparing business plans for entrepreneurs. If anyone knows of someone who could use our help, please have them contact me."

I listened intently as chamber members used infomercial time to promote their businesses—what a great way to promote your business and get to know people in the community. I recognized a few faces from the Rotary Club meetings, eliciting a feeling of belonging and a connection to my new community. Neither Jennifer nor I were winners of the 50–50! Oh well, maybe next time.

At the end of the meeting, I asked Jennifer if she had a few minutes to talk?

"Sure. What do you need?"

I got right into my relationship question, asking Jennifer her take on Albert, Hannah, and Sara.

Jennifer said, "The three young people did know each other, and yes, Albert and Hannah had been a couple ever since high school, even though they had not lived together, were inseparable, had lots of friends, and were real party-goers. On the surface, Sara was outgoing enough. It was a mystery to me why she hadn't connected personally with anyone over the years, not in high school, in college, or even her adult life as a business owner, for that matter." Jennifer confirmed what Tim had said, "Sara was always on the outside looking in. Whether by choice, Jennifer did not know."

Jennifer's thoughtful final comments summed up her understanding of the Sara she knew. "Maggie, I used to see Sara at most of the community events I attended, and we were members of many of the same business organizations, including the Chamber of Commerce. I worked with Sara on several committees over the years, but she was always reserved, making it hard for people to get to know her. A real puzzle!"

Thinking over what Jennifer said, I felt sorry for the dead woman and offered, "Sara must have led a very lonely life; I now understood why Sara had flipped out over Trip's rejection. He may have been the only person in her life with whom she had made a small personal connection. Sara did not understand that casual dating did not always end in a meaningful full-time relationship. She must have felt dejected, perhaps even, God forbid, suicidal when Trip ended it."

Jennifer replied, "I sincerely hope that was not the case."

"On the subject of relationships, Jennifer," Trip asked me out on an official date next Saturday evening."

Jennifer, beaming, said, "It is about time!"

"Jennifer, I am worried that I am not quite emotionally ready to share what happened last year."

Something in Jennifer's kindhearted demeanor spurred me one, and I confessed, "Trip, and I do not know much about each other's past. Once we are alone, we need to start revealing personal information. Talking about my mother's death and leaving my hotel GM job might send me back into a depressed state."

In response, Jennifer reached over and hugged me, saying, "I am sure Trip will understand if you need more time. Trip has his own sad story that he needs to share with you, but I will let him tell you about that. It seems that you both will benefit from sharing."

Jennifer thought for a moment before adding, "I believe in the old proverb, *a trouble shared is a trouble halved*, and I am confident that the two of you will sort this out."

Jennifer glanced at her watch, saying, "I am out of time. I have to get back to the office to finalize some contracts before I go home for the day."

"Thanks for taking time out of your busy day to help me sort through the relationships between Albert, Hannah, and Sara. I especially appreciate your listening to my concerns about Trip and my relationship."

"I am glad we were able to get together today, Maggie. I, too, need a friend to help me sort things through from time to time. You are not only fun to be with but level headed! I am always around my adult children, but that is not the same as having a woman friend you can trust!"

"Thanks for the kind words, Jennifer. I love being in your company and would be honored to be a sounding board for you!"

We hugged each other again and parted company.

I drove home, mulling over my conversation with Jennifer. I must admit I feel much better after talking to Jennifer about Trip. I value Jennifer's friendship, and with my mother gone, I need a close friend, and Jennifer could be that person. The ability to form relationships within my community and with coworkers is essential to deciding whether I should permanently settle down in River Town.

Chapter Twenty-Seven

I woke up Saturday morning realizing that it was our first official date night. I knew Trip would not pass up the opportunity to kid me about that. I honestly was excited about tonight. I quickly climbed out of bed, trying not to step on Lily, who was sitting on the floor waiting impatiently for food. She followed me to the kitchen, overseeing my attempt to fill her food dish and refresh her water. With Lilly taken care of, I could now make a coffee.

The day seemed to drag; I tried to stay busy with my usual household chores and a little light reading. I was ready in plenty of time for my date and sat in the living room waiting. I was elated when I finally heard Trip's car pull into the driveway and watched him climb the front porch steps from the living room window.

He rang the doorbell, Lily and I greeted him at the door. Trip impeccably dressed in a black suit, a freshly starched white shirt, and a retro purple striped tie looked quite dashing, and I told him so! Hugging me, he told Lily her hug and strokes would have to wait; black suits and cat fur don't quite mix.

Trip glancing admiringly at my mid-length, emerald green satin form-fitting dress, pearl accessories, and color-coordinated high heels, helped me into my matching emerald green jacket, saying, "You look gorgeous, Maggie." I was pleased by his reaction smiled up at him, saying, "Thank you."

I picked up my purse and keys from the coffee table and handed Trip my keys; after locking the front door, he returned them, and I tucked them in my purse.

We walked down the porch steps— opening the car door for me, Trip formerly addressing me said, "Ms. McManus, just in case you are unsure, at this moment, we are on an official date, and I can't think of anyone I would rather be going out with."

Looking up at Trip with a wicked grin, my flirty response, "Thank goodness, I thought you would never officially ask me out," elicited the hoped-for laughter.

Once we were on the road, Trip finally told me we were going to Skippers, a fine dining restaurant in Pembroke. Skippers, located on Pond Street, had fantastic reviews. He said he had searched high and low for a restaurant that offered dancing but could not find one in our area.

I confided that I had never been to any of the well-known restaurants on Pond Street, nor had I explored the surrounding beach area and all that it had to offer.

I awkwardly confessed that one of the downsides of teaching is you spend most of your time with students and limited time interacting with your adult teaching counterparts. Although admittedly, I now have many acquaintances through Rotary Club and Chamber affiliations, I had yet to make any, what I would consider, close friends other than Jennifer.

"How about me? I hope you consider me a friend?"

I felt terrible about that misstep and replied, "Oh dear, Trip, of course, you are. I consider you one of the best friends I have ever had!"

Trip quietly replied, "Thanks, Maggie. I am sure you will add to your list of friends once you have lived in River Town longer. I met Jennifer and her family through the Chamber of Commerce. I will forever be grateful I'm included in their inner circle. You have just become a part of that circle, and in time, trust me; you will come to love them all as much as I do. Personally, Maggie, I do not need many friends, just a few good ones."

I changed the subject and voiced my concern about leaving Lily by herself that evening.

Trip attempted to reassure me, saying, "Lily will be OK and undoubtedly appreciating you more when you return; after all, Maggie, it has been said, 'Absence makes the heart grow fonder.'" I replied without hesitation, "I don't believe that for a minute, absence from loved ones has always made me feel just plain lonely."

I knew I was stepping out in faith when I decided to clarify my negative-sounding statement. "My father died in a car accident when I was three, and I still mourn that loss. Growing up without a father, I depended totally on my mother. When Mom died last year, I was devastated. Even after extensive bereavement counseling, I still can't get past her death. I miss her terribly."

"I remember you telling me your mother moved in with you after she retired."

"Yes, she did, Trip, but sadly, that was because she became quite ill and could no longer live on her own."

"What caused her death, Maggie?"

I tensed up but replied, "Mom had cancer, and they found it too late to treat." I was struggling to talk about my mother's death, but I continued. "In the end, Mom was in Hospice Care, and someone needed to be with her round the clock. I took the night shift and then some.

"On the day Mom died, my secretary called me to tell me about a critical situation at the hotel. There was a Hospice employee on duty, and since Mom was sleeping, I decided to go to the hotel and handle it. I returned in less than two hours. During my absence, Mom passed away. I will never forgive myself for leaving her that day."

I was sitting very still with tears streaming down my cheeks. Pulling the car into a storefront parking lot, Trip turned off the engine and slid out from under the wheel. He brought me into his arms, stroking my back, kissing my cheeks, saying,

"You are a brave woman, and you will be alright. No one could fault you for leaving your mom that day. Your mom was in good hands.

"Maggie, if you knew it was your mother's last day, you would never have left her, but rarely does anyone have that kind of insight. It might have been harder on your mother if you had been home, and she had to say goodbye to you. Perhaps she did not want your remembrance of her to be viewing her last dying breath."

Trip continued, "Your mom would want you to move on and would be scolding you for blaming yourself, Maggie. Who knows what kind of guilt she may have been carrying for not having cancer screening done regularly, blaming herself for not having more time with you?"

Releasing me, Trip handed me a tissue from the consul to wipe the tears from my face.

I had been listening and internalizing everything Trip said. Looking up at him, I mustered a smile quietly, saying, "You are right. Mom kept telling me how badly she felt about not being screened for cancer. She admittedly ignored that she wasn't feeling good and knew something was wrong. My mother expected great things from me. She had made a considerable investment of herself in me and would be devastated if she thought her death interfered in my living my life to its fullest."

I decided to forge on, "Mom knew I loved hotels but wanted to work with young people, and she was pleased that I was applying for teaching jobs. I am glad I started doing that while she was still alive. She also knew I loved children and hoped I would marry and have a family. I had been seeing someone for several years, and he told me he wanted to marry me but had no desire for a family.

I had no idea just how selfish Edward was until my mother needed me, and I asked her to move in. He maintained that with my mother living with me, I wasn't available for a relationship, and he broke up with me.

Trip reached over, pulled me back into his arms, hugging me close to him—"Edwards's loss. I am grateful that you shared your story about your mother's death with me; that means you trust me. I am so sorry for your loss, Maggie."

Trip released me and moved back behind the wheel. Checking his watch, he said, "Are you OK to get back on the road?"

"Yes, I am. Thank you for listening, Trip."

"Any time, Maggie and I truly mean that!"

We arrived at Skippers a few minutes before our 6:00 p.m. reservation. The hostess showed us to our table and presented us with menus. I promptly excused myself to freshen up. When I returned, Trip told me the waiter had been by and recommended the evenings featured white wine—Barnett Vineyards, San Giacomo Carneros. Not knowing your preference, I asked him to come back.

I told Trip I prefer white wines regardless of my main meal. Trip replied he was on board with white and would order a bottle of the featured wine.

Laughing, I told Trip, "I never dated anyone I could talk to about the ladies' room décor before. The room is beautifully decorated, and the high-end amenities are impressive!"

With that said, we both looked around the dining room, admiring the impeccably set tables covered with crisp white linen table cloths, blue napkins, vases of fresh flowers, and highly polished silverware.

The Skipper dining room theme, true to its name, was upscale nautical. A beautiful mermaid artform hung on the main wall surrounded by colorful seahorses. The floor-to-ceiling woven fabric sea-green drapes reflective of the Emerald Coast waters added a relaxing atmosphere to the room.

I opened my menu and went straight to the seafood section. The waiter returned, took our wine order, and asked if we were ready to order?

Trip said, "I had a chance to look while you were in the ladies' room. Don't let me sway you, but I have decided on a Caesar Salad and Scamp Cervantes."

"The Seared Red Snapper sounds wonderful, and I too would like a Caesar Salad."

Shortly after the waiter took our orders, a basket of rolls and a butter dish with cloverleaf-shaped pats of butter arrived at the table. We selected croissants from the basket, placing them and a pat of butter on our bread plates.

Trip began buttering his roll and, without looking up, said, "Thank you for trusting me and sharing your story about your mother."

"In all sincerity, I can't tell you how freeing it was to tell you what happened."

Changing the subject, I asked, "Trip, what was it like growing up as an only child in your family?"

"I was very close to my parents. Their world revolved around me. They seemed determined to make sure I had the best education, fun-filled summer vacations, music, and dance lessons. They even attended parent-teacher conferences together. Both my parents worked, but they always made sure I was cared for by a responsible, loving nanny. I always knew I was loved and love them both dearly."

"How about you, Maggie?" Trip asked.

"Well, as I mentioned, my dad died when I was three, so my mother was my rock. Mom was an only child, too, and her parents died at a young age. I had some close friends in high school, but we lost touch when we left home for college. So, it was pretty much just Mom and me for most of my life.

"Like your parents, my mother was high on education, but then she was an elementary school teacher. As a teacher, she had summers off, but she took on extra jobs tutoring students or waiting tables to bring in extra money.

"I think the extra-curricular activities like the dance lessons and violin were meant to keep me busy and out of trouble. I didn't have much in the way of free time. When I reached my high school years, I too worked summers, waiting tables. One summer, I worked as a chambermaid in a guest house on Cape Cod. Mom didn't want me to go, but I wanted to try my wings."

The waiter returned with our bottle of wine. Uncorking the bottle, he poured a small amount in a long stem glass and handed Trip the glass. Trip held the glass up to the light to evaluate its color and clarity; swirling the wine in the glass to aerate and release its aroma, he smelled the wine approving the subtle scent. Tasting the wine, Trip declared, "Fit for consumption."

The waiter topped off Trip's glass and poured one for me. We touched glasses; Trip offered the Italian toast, "Salute," meaning cheers. We sat quietly, enjoying the wine, the ambiance, and just being together.

The beautifully presented salads arrived, prompting Trip to comment before savoring his first bite, "It is so refreshing to be dining with someone who appreciates the same things I do." The seafood dishes were both equally impressive in presentation and taste. As we oohed and aahed our way through them, sharing samples of food, Trip commented, "We sound like little children!"

Trip refilled our wine glasses, and I proposed a toast, "May we always find the wonder and enjoyment in beautiful life experiences."

"Agreed," Trip responded.

Our waiter returned, asking, "Any interest in dessert?"

I looked at Trip for a sign, none coming. I answered, "No, thank you. I have no room."

Trip echoed my response, and the Waiter cleared our plates and returned with the check and two foil-wrapped mints. Naturally, I offered to help pay. To which Trip replied, "I asked you out, my treat!"

"Thank you so much for an incredible dining experience, Trip."

We left Skippers with a full stomach and a deep appreciation for the restaurant's excellent food, service, and overall ambiance. We were back in the car headed to River Town by 7:30 p.m.

On the way back, Trip asked, "Maggie, would you like to come to my place for a nightcap or coffee? I want to show you where I live and give you the grand tour of my historic old house." With no hesitation, I replied, "I would love a house tour, some coffee, and a chance to see Sally and Harry again." I knew this was a significant step in our relationship. I sat smiling in the darkness; after our rocky start this evening, life holds promise.

Harry and Sally were nowhere around when we arrived. Trip showed me around the house, and we found them sound asleep on his bed. Not ready to get up for anyone, we left them sleeping and went into the kitchen.

Trip's home was about as opposite of mine as you could get. He lives in a beautifully restored, charming old colonial with many bedrooms, bathrooms, and gathering rooms. A perfect family home, I thought and told him so.

While Trip brewed coffee, I sat at the kitchen table, admiring his beautifully restored colonial kitchen. I couldn't refuse a piece of the River Town Bakery cherry pie he offered, and Trip cut two small slices to help with our guilt.

We sat at the kitchen table eating pie and sipping coffee; it felt like we had been doing this for years. We talked about Trip's neighborhood, his walk to work that morning, and how he had found the house with Jennifer's help. And then Trip asked, "Would you like to hear my sad family story?"

I told him, "I would."

Trip began by saying," I was married to a woman who loved the glamour of being the wife of a hotel manager. Sissy was a stay-at-home wife with no desire for a career. She wanted to attend parties and hobnob with people who had titles, money, and influence. As you know, hotel general managers attend galas and the like, but more often than not, we end up handling problems at events held at our properties. Sissy felt she should come before any crisis that arose. She accused me of spending too much time at the hotel and didn't understand why I was always on call.

"Shortly after we were married, Sissy told me that, under the circumstances, with all the hours I spent at work, a family was out of the question; she would be raising them alone and had never wanted children anyway.

"Our marriage was short-lived, two years almost to the day. I came home from work one day, and Sissy had packed her bags. She told me she had already told my parents she was leaving me; they were devastated and blamed me. I was shocked and embarrassed, and it took a while before I could finally divulge the truth to my parents that Sissy had been cheating on me and had found someone new. Sissy remarried three months after our divorce.

"However, that revelation seemed to fall on deaf ears. My parents didn't feel differently about her; I was the guilty one. Mom still insisted that Sissy divorced me because I left her alone too much. Dad, well, he just shrugged his shoulders, saying he hoped Sissy's new husband would make her happy.

" I felt betrayed by my parents, hurt beyond belief. I used to call my parents almost daily. After the divorce, they always began our conversations with, 'Have you heard from Sissy?' Never about how I was doing. I finally just stopped calling. Mom started leaving weekly messages on my phone, urging me to call her back. I hurt too much and couldn't do that; they refused to look at Sissy's role in the divorce and blamed me instead. Sissy was always the subject of our conversations.

"I needed to regroup and figure out what to do with myself. Finally, I found another hotel GM position in Michigan. I was there for four years and moved to River Town to start this job six months ago. I haven't spoken to my parents in many years. Mom stopped calling, and they communicated by sending cards for my birthday and Christmas."

After that unburdening, Trip sat quietly, obviously thinking things through. He finally continued saying, "Maggie, listening to you talk about your mother and your relationship with Edward has convinced me I need to put on a new pair of glasses and look at my situation from a different perspective.

"Admittedly, I was relieved when Sissy left; we had nothing in common. My parents, on the other hand, deserved more from me. I should have stayed in touch with them regardless of Sissy. I should never have let her come between us. I am going to make every effort, starting tomorrow, to reach out to them and mend fences."

When Trip finished, I softly said, "It is hard to know what is in the hearts and minds of others unless you are willing to ask them, even if you are fearful of the answers. Sissy said, your parents blamed you, but that was before you told them the truth. I could almost see why they initially thought she was the victim."

Trip woefully replied, "I am beginning to see that my feelings of inadequacy surrounding the divorce were the real issue. My inability to converse openly and honestly with my parents caused the rift. They kept reaching out; I closed the door."

Intuitively I replied, "I suspect they didn't know what to say to you and perhaps hoped you would fill in the gaps. Asking about Sissy didn't mean they didn't care about you. She had been part of your life for two years, even if she had moved on. I am sure they had no idea what Sissy's leaving meant to you. I think reaching out to them is a wonderful idea; having an open and honest conversation about Sissy is a good starting point."

"Thanks for listening, Maggie. I wasn't sure how to bring up the subject of my parents. Listening to you talk about your mom's passing helped me broach the subject of my parents. I feel so much better after sharing my story with you, and you are right; I never did tell them what Sissy's leaving meant to me."

I responded by telling Trip that Jennifer had quoted the idiom: "A trouble shared is a trouble halved." Jennifer confided she thought discussing problems with loved ones, people who care for us, can help us reduce the burden. "I think we both just found that out for ourselves, Trip."

Looking at my watch, I said, "I can't believe it is 10:30 p.m. I am feeling guilty about leaving Lily for so long. I had better get home."

Trip put the dishes in the dishwasher before we headed out the front door.

"Oh my gosh, Trip, do you realize we didn't even talk about the murders this evening?"

"You're right, Maggie. Imagine what our lives will be like once these murders are solved!"

Trip drove me home, walked me to my front door, and stood there, just looking down at me. He finally spoke, "Maggie, I am speechless. I had such a wonderful evening on so many fronts. I could never properly put into words what this evening means to me. All I know is, I am the happiest I have been in my entire life." With that, he bent down, wrapped me in his arms, and kissed me. The passion he was feeling was unmistakable, and I was responding in kind. We clung to each other, kissing for what seemed like an eternity.

Finally, I pulled free, gasping for breath, saying, "I hope we can continue this another time."

Trip took my keys, opened the door for me, and let me slip inside, but not before saying, "I will call you tomorrow, and rest assured, I will be counting the minutes till we can pick up where we left off."

Wow, what a night! A cold shower, and I would be in bed soon dreaming about my spectacular date with Trip Evans. Lily was sound asleep on my bed and, like Sally and Harry, had no intention of waking up just because I had come home. And I was worried, why?

Chapter Twenty-Eight

T rip called me Sunday morning, once again saying he truly felt his date with me last night was the best night in his life; ever. Bubbling over with enthusiasm, I told Trip I, too, had had a wonderful time, thanking him profusely for the elegant romantic dinner at Skippers. I told him I truly appreciated him taking me to his house for dessert, adding, "I love your home; it has warm and cozy vibes; it is a larger version of the home I lived in with my mother in New England."

I went on to say, "I couldn't wait to tell you that I woke up this morning feeling a wonderful sense of well-being. At long last, I think the demons from my past are gone— you helped me see that I was needlessly carrying guilt about my mother's death."

Trip said he felt the same way about sharing his story with me and that he was going to call his parents later in the day. He abruptly changed gears saying, "Maggie, I have to go; the front desk just told me there is a situation at the desk I need to handle. I will call you later," and he hung up.

I sat, thinking about my conversation with Trip. I hope one day soon I will get to meet Trip's parents. After all, we discovered last evening that family was important to both of us. Who knows, if our relationship continues to blossom, having a family might still be a consideration.

I hope Trip's emergency isn't another death at the hotel. Our relationship always comes back around to who killed Hannah and Sara. It would be lovely if we had the luxury of just working on moving our relationship forward. We aren't getting any younger, and time was of the essence if having a family is to be a consideration.

I retrieved my "murder file" from the filing cabinet; how quickly the details can get away from me. We needed to figure out when Sara left the hotel the day Hannah was murdered. Hopefully, the tapes would hold the answer to that question, but what possible motive would Sara have for killing Hannah?

Then there was the question of Albert's presence in the hotel the night of Sara's murder. Did Albert know Mark, the bartender, would be on duty or Sara would be there? His appearance was still suspect. Coincidental? I sincerely doubt that. Albert knew his way around the hotel and could have gone into the board room. Viewing the tapes was paramount to learning the whereabouts of these two people on the days of both murders. It was also critical to find out who was in the bar the night Sara died.

Just out of curiosity, I decided to google Albert Smith. I found a newspaper article about his recent arrest containing his home address. Albert lived in the town of Barry, not too far from the downtown area of River Town. I googled "Barry, Florida" and discovered that Barry had its start in 1845 when Richard Barry, a settler, established a sawmill there. A post office called Barry had been in operation since 1889.

I knew it was probably not a good idea, but I grabbed my purse, car keys, and cell phone. I sat in my car, entered Albert's address in my GPS, and set out to find his house. If nothing else, I thought, a day's outing to a nearby community purported to be charming and historical might be enjoyable.

How people choose to live speaks volumes about who they are and what they value. Barry, I discovered, is a community of carefully restored older homes, preserving the area's architecture, culture, and history. However, other sections of town with run-down houses reflected poorly on the community.

Albert had opted to live in a section of town that welcomed anyone who had no desire to maintain their property or lawns. Albert's house turned out to be a small bungalow— brutal honesty; it is nothing more than a shack with a front porch and yard filled with junk of all kinds. I couldn't help thinking Albert was either a hoarder or just an average *run-of-the-mill* slob! I hadn't met the man but couldn't help asking myself why Hannah had spent twenty years of her life in a relationship with someone whose values were clearly on display in the deplorable condition of his home. For all her faults, Hannah should have been able to find a better suitor than Albert. No wonder her parents were dead set against this relationship, beside themselves, when it continued into her adulthood.

I parked across the street for quite some time, leaving the car running, staring at Albert's dilapidated house, thinking about Hannah. While I was sitting there, a car pulled into the driveway, and a tall, skinny disheveled man with long, stringy, dirty blond hair got out on the passenger side. It must be Albert. The driver drove off, and Albert sensing something, perhaps intuitively feeling someone watching him, looked around the yard and then across the street to see me sitting in my car. I had never seen Albert before, and he certainly would have no idea who I was, but parking across from his house would raise his suspicions.

We eyeballed each other, leaving me frightened beyond belief, jamming the car in gear; I rapidly drove away. Whew! My hands were shaking so badly; I had to hang on to the steering wheel for dear life to help calm me down. I sped toward home, hoping that Albert hadn't gotten my license plate number, enabling him to find out who I was.

Returning home, I discovered I had missed a call from Trip. It was now 2:30 p.m., and I dialed his number intending to confess that I had been out stalking Albert. Trip was a bit out of sorts himself, and I decided to tell him tomorrow.

Trip started our conversation by telling me about his morning emergency. Saying, "Nothing too critical, but unhappy guests are bad for business. When I got to the front desk, I found a boisterous older couple standing there refuting breakfast charges on their bill, insisting they had only eaten two breakfasts at the hotel and the charges were for three. A small group of people had gathered, listening intently to the couple's complaint. I took the two of them back to my office, and after reviewing the three breakfast charges and discussing what they had eaten at each meal, they sheepishly admitted they were wrong and left."

Trip then got to the main reason for his call and told me about his conversation with his parents that morning. After Sissy's divorce from Abigail's father, he learned that she had brought Abigail to visit his parents a few times. I asked Dad if he knew why Sissy divorced her second husband? Mom chimed in, saying, "He was unhappy that she was having a baby. Sissy said her husband started cheating on her once he found out she was pregnant."

"Frankly, Maggie, I am embarrassed I succumbed, but I couldn't resist saying, 'Mom, it sounds like poetic justice to me. Why weren't you and Dad outraged at Sissy when she cheated on me with Abigail's father while she was married to me! Sissy was the one saying she never wanted children!' Neither of them responded to my outburst!"

Taking a stand with his parents about his ex-wife had clearly left him agitated, and I sympathetically said, "It must have been a difficult phone call, Trip."

He slid past my remark, saying, "On the bright side, Maggie, my parents have agreed to come for a visit next month. I have been thinking about having a housewarming party. This gathering would be a great opportunity for my parents to get involved in my life instead of Sissy's."

"Love your thinking, Trip; I would be more than happy to help."

With that, the conversation ended.

I sat staring at my watch 10/21, 6:30 a.m. Today is when outlines and blueprints from my two Monday classes are due. This week, I will be spending considerable time reviewing project submissions and providing each group with extensive constructive criticism.

I was relieved that I had already prepared for both of today's classes. No doubt, I would have had a hard time concentrating on lesson planning this morning. I couldn't stop worrying about Albert seeing me parked in front of his house yesterday. Scary, especially if he found out who I was and he turned out to be a murderer. I would call the police, but what could Detectives Callahan and Barker do? I was the one stalking Albert!

My much-needed walk would have to wait. First things first, Lily was looking for food. I left Lily crunching on Purina Kitten Nuggets, made myself a cup of coffee, and dialed Trip's home phone. Time to confess about going in search of Albert yesterday. Trip was sure to be upset, maybe even angry that I foolishly put myself in danger. The sound of Trip's bright, good morning sent a wave of relief through my body. Feeling somewhat unnerved, I knew my voice must have sounded shaky when I said, "Trip, is this a bad time for you to talk? I need to tell you something." Trip responded, "Maggie, what's wrong?"

As my story of searching for Albert unfolded, it reminded me what a dumb thing I had done, and I told Trip so.

Trip never passed judgment, saying, "I wish you had called to let me know what you were up to; I would have tried to change up my day and gone with you." Trip echoed my concern about Albert figuring out who I was and trying to harm me. Contacting the detectives before we finished our investigation didn't seem like a good idea, either.

We agreed that we needed to justify meddling in police matters and withholding information from Barker and Callahan. If we had something concrete to tell them, the detectives might take pity on us.

Viewing the back door tapes was a top priority. Now that I knew what Albert looked like, we could re-check the front door video from the day of Sara's murder to see if Albert left the bar around the time Sara did. Mark, the bartender knew who else was at the bar the night of Sara's death; another meeting with Mark was in order. Time was of the essence; we needed answers before Albert found out I had been watching his house!

"I am going to review the bar checks once again to see if anyone's name pops up that might have a relationship with one or both of the women. I initially only looked at the bar checks to determine who had bought the wine that killed Sara."

"Good idea, Trip."

We made arrangements to meet early the following day to view the hotel's back entrance tapes for the days of both murders. Trip ended the call saying, "Please be careful, Maggie, do not answer your door unless you know who's there."

Chapter Twenty-Nine

E ven though I felt jumpy, I managed to get through both classes, continually looking over my shoulder to see if Albert had found me. I was glad when my last class ended, and I could return to the comfort of my home and Lily.

I had a terrible time getting to sleep and spent most of the night tossing and turning. Lily sensing my restlessness, had opted to sleep on the sofa. I had finally gotten to sleep when the alarm sounded at 6 a.m.

Coffee and a light breakfast would have to do today. Dressing quickly in a pair of black slacks and a white turtle-neck sweater, I slipped into black low riser boots.

My hair ended up in a ponytail, not one of my better fashion statement days. My outside appearance was not the priority; getting to the hotel to begin viewing the tapes with Trip was. I was halfway out the door when I remembered I had not put on any makeup or earrings. Oh well, I chuckled; how important is that on a scale of one to ten? Bottom of the list or not on it. My counselor would be proud of me!

I checked in at the front desk with Angela, and she called Trip's cell phone to tell him I had arrived. Trip met me in the lobby, saying, "I suspect it is going to be a long morning; let's stop by the dining room to pick up some fortification." Trip carried the tray containing coffee fixings and two blueberry muffins to the security office, with me following close behind, watching Trip artfully carrying the tray. Another reminder about something else we shared, the love of coffee.

We settled into the security office, and Trip poured coffee. Handing me a cup, he commenced telling me he had spent quite a bit of time the previous day conducting a tedious check sorting process, sorting bar checks by payment method, cash, credit card, and house charges.

Hotel guests charge food and beverage from the hotel's restaurants and bars to their rooms, but the chances of anyone staying at the hotel being the killer were slim, but no stone should be left unturned, he told me. One of those guests might have witnessed something happening regarding Sara in the bar that night. Sorting the credit card charges by shift would also help identify who might have been in the bar while Sara was there. He had set aside the cash checks since there was no way of determining who paid those charges.

"The night shift starts at 5 p.m. Mark, the bartender, told me Albert was the only person in the bar with a connection to Sara that evening. Albert's departure from the bar shortly after Sara was suspect. Curiously, though, since Mark indicated he and Albert were long-time friends, how noble of Mark to share a timeframe that set Albert up as a possible suspect!"

Trip sounded discouraged when he admitted, "Maggie, after all that work, I discovered there really were not that many people in the bar when Sara was. And worse, none of the names on the credit cards were familiar to me, other than Sara's. If all else fails, the detectives might have to contact those house guests to find out what was happening in the bar that evening."

I suspected Trip hadn't slept well last night, and he told me he hadn't. He had arrived at the hotel at 7:30 a.m. and had already cued up the back door's tapes for the morning of Hannah's murder. We started reviewing the recordings from 8 a.m., watching the employees coming and going through the back entrance. Trip remarked, "I should know the identity of anyone using this employee entrance. A nonemployee will stick out like a sore thumb."

Bartender Mark made an appearance entering the back door at 9 a.m., leaving at 10:50 a.m. "Why was he there?" I asked Trip, "Isn't he a night shift employee?"

Trip thought for a minute before saying, "Yes, and the only reason I can think of is to take inventory or to stock the bar. I can check his timecard and see if he punched in, but the timing sure is suspect."

We decided to focus on Hannah's death first. Now that I knew what Albert looked like, we needed to go back and look for him entering or exiting the hotel via the front door. Trip cued up the tapes from the front door, starting at 8 a.m. on the day of Hannah's death. We knew Sara had come through the front door that morning and had not left through the employee's back door. She must have departed via the front door, and we needed to view an expanded timeline to see what time she left the hotel.

We viewed the footage in its entirety from 8 a.m. until 12 p.m. Trip fast-forwarding through parts where there was little or no activity. Albert never showed up. Sara, however, was finally seen leaving the hotel at 11:10 a.m. Where had she been from 10:15 a.m. when she left the Young Professional's meeting until departing the hotel at 11:10 a.m.? Her timing was also suspect.

It took the better part of the morning to view this footage. I told Trip I needed to take a break, go home to check on Lily, answer email messages, and have a quick lunch.

Trip agreed, saying, "I should check my email and see if the desk has taken any messages for me."

I told Trip I would be back at 1 p.m. to continue the search.

I half expected to find Albert waiting for me outside the hotel and was relieved when I made it home and back to the hotel at 1 p.m. without any sign of him. Trip cued up the day of Sara's murder, and we began looking at the front entrance starting at 5 p.m. Once again, we searched for Albert Smith, Sara, and anyone else who might be considered suspect in either Sara's or Hannah's murders. Sara arrived at 5:40 p.m. and headed in the direction of the restaurant service bar. We fast-forwarded through the tapes up until 7 p.m. Albert did not show up, nor did anyone else of any interest.

Next, we began searching the back-door footage from 5 p.m. Trip was dumbfounded when shortly after 5:35 p.m., I identified the person entering the employee entrance as Albert. After looking around to see if anyone noticed him, Albert, heading in the general direction of the hotel lobby and the restaurant service bar.

Trip slammed his fist on the table, saying, "Albert had no business using that entrance; employees are issued security cards for that entrance. A new system I implemented long after Albert left the hotel's employ. Someone breached our security system. Probably Hannah, as she had little respect for authority, and as a manager, she would have been able to authorize a card for him."

Albert's arrival supported what Mark, the bartender, had told us; Albert had entered the bar shortly before Sara. Now we needed to determine what time Albert left the hotel. Mark told me he left the bar shortly after Sara, so it was critical to learn if he had followed her to the boardroom or left the hotel. We picked him up on tape, leaving the hotel via the hotel's back entrance at 6:00 p.m. We knew that Sara ended up in the boardroom around 5:55 p.m. Unless Albert returned at a later time, he was technically off the hook.

We did not want to review these back door tapes again, so we stayed the course fast-forwarding through the videos until 9 p.m. There were no further signs of Albert entering or leaving the hotel, and thank goodness everyone else seemed to be a current employee. Trip straightened up the security office and put the security tapes in a box. We took the box of tapes back to Trips office and sat mulling over the day's findings.

Albert seemed to be in the clear for physically committing both murders. Trip would have to talk to the police department about Albert breaching the hotel's security; rekeying the hotel would be costly. Sara had the opportunity to kill Hannah. Mark was at the hotel during the time of both murders. Unless we came up with a motive for either of these people, we were nowhere; just speculation about relationship issues when they were all teenagers, but no concrete proof that anything happened that would drive someone to kill.

We sat there thinking about what we might be missing, and suddenly Trip announced, "There were numerous people in the hotel during the time both murders took place—guests and employees alike. We know that many employees had it in for Hannah. It's possible an employee who was working a shift in the hotel could have killed her."

I added, "We would not necessarily have viewed their coming and going from the employee entrance in the time frames we searched. I still think there is a problem here; what about Sara's murder? Why would an employee kill Sara too? It is doubtful that the deaths of two women in the same room two weeks apart were coincidental."

Trip noted, "Houseguests were also already inside the hotel. Hannah could have had a confrontation with any of them. And after murdering her, they could have just gone back to their room. Was it a stretch to think there might be any correlation between Hannah, Sara, and either a house guest or an employee? We need to know who the registered hotel guests are on the days Hannah and Sara died."

Trip called the front desk and asked for a printout of the guestlist for both days. Checking payroll records to determine which employees worked both days would require a bit more work, and he would have Human Resources help him with that the following day.

We sat anxiously awaiting the front desk reports. Trip said he didn't hold out much hope that the hotel guest lists would turn up anything, but it was worth a try. At the very least, he could turn the reports over to the police detectives if they didn't turn up anything meaningful to us. "Maggie, surprisingly, the detectives never asked me who was in-house the day of the murders."

"Well, why the heck not? No way to run a railroad, never mind a murder investigation," I retorted.

Trip, naturally, agreed.

The call we were sitting on the edge of our seats waiting for finally came. Trip hurried out of the office, returning in less than a minute. He handed me one of the lists, and we began scanning the names.

Trip's report was for the day Hannah died. After looking it over, he tossed his list on the table, disappointment written all over his face—there weren't any names on it that rang any bells.

I drew a deep breath, looking at Trip wide-eyed, saying, "Trip, this is odd; Susan Milligan, Sara's sister, is on my list.

We discovered Sara's body on Sunday. Susan checked into the hotel the Friday before the murder and left on Sunday. I wonder what she was doing in town?" "According to Bart, Sara's lawyer," Trip interjected, "Susan would have known she was going to inherit Sara's estate by then. Had she coincidentally come the day before the murder with the intent of patching things up with Sara?

"Maggie, Bart, and I were talking about the hotel, and he brought up Sara's death, saying he had called Susan to tell her about Sara's death. That couldn't have been any earlier than Monday, and Susan could have been back home by then. Bart hadn't mentioned Susan being in-town that weekend; he may not have known."

All this left us with even more questions, and I pondered out loud, "I wonder if Susan contacted Sara to tell her she was in town? Is it possible that Sara and Susan had planned on meeting in the bar and why she had not gone straight to the Ball?"

"That would certainly make sense. However, if Susan was at the bar, we know she did not leave when Sara did."

"Trip, we don't know what Susan looks like, so we might not have connected her as one of the people who left the bar after Sara, but why would she have left later?"

"True, and Maggie, Susan, and Sara must have gone to the same schools; was it possible that Mark knew Susan? If so, and Susan was in the bar the night that Sara died, why wouldn't he have mentioned it?"

"That is a fair question. Trip, I give up! I think it is time to turn this over to Barker and Callahan."

Trip never said a word while I rambled on; his shocked expression said it all.

"This is way beyond us; we do not have the resources to pursue this further. Too many loose ends and so many questions that need answering! We could damage the investigation if we tip our hand and begin asking Albert, Mark, or Susan questions about their involvement in either of the deaths.

"Something else, to consider Trip, we are not even sure the security guard who failed to inspect the rooms isn't part of the equation. And why did the Superintendent of schools not tell us that Sara and Albert were in a close relationship for twenty years instead of calling it harassment? Who was the boy who asked Sara to the prom who had been carrying a grudge for years? Is that important? What, if anything, did the newspaper article in Hannah's file have to do with any of this; it tied Hannah to Albert and Mark but was there anything more to the missing money and credit card fraud that we could not turn up?

"Also, Albert might try to find out who I am; I might need police protection! If we continue, besides undermining the investigation, even worse, we could be putting our relationship, not to mention our lives, in jeopardy; nothing is worth that."

When I appeared to be through, Trip replied, "Maggie, Maggie, Maggie, you are amazing. I was thinking the same things and was trying to find a way to tell you. I was afraid you might think my wanting to turn this over to the detectives was a shortcoming in my personality; that I was giving up too easily."

"To the contrary, Trip, it is important to know one's limits. We have reached ours."

Trip laughed, saying, "In the words of Kenny Rogers, *know when to fold 'em.*"

After deciding that our investigating days were over, we sat in silence for a few minutes. Trip spoke first, saying, "Any ideas about how we should handle telling Barker and Callahan?"

"I do. We should call Callahan and ask him to come to the hotel tomorrow morning, while this is all fresh in our minds. But before we do that, we should write up a factual account of what we have learned about both murders. At some point, we might need to give individual statements. Writing it down together will reinforce what we have learned and keep our stories straight. Callahan might try to trip us up, and it would be helpful if our facts and recollections of all events are the same."

Trip sensing I was as exhausted as he was, asked, "Do you want to push on and write up the report today? We could put it off until very early tomorrow morning?"

My one-word response, "Today."

Back in Trip's office, we began the grueling task of documenting everything we had discovered about both murders.

Trip sat in front of his computer, typing up our collective thoughts. It was almost 7 p.m. when we finally finished.

Trip picked up the phone and dialed Callahan's number. We did not expect him to answer and planned on leaving him a message. Callahan answering the phone threw us off guard. Trip asked Callahan if he could come to the hotel the following morning at 9 a.m.?

Callahan, the man of a few words, asked, "Why?" Trip told him we wanted to talk to him about Hannah's and Sara's murders. We have information we think will be helpful to you. Callahan's curt reply before hanging up, "See you tomorrow."

"Whew, glad we settled that. I need to get home, Trip, and I am sure you do too. I will see you tomorrow at 8:45 a.m."

Trip replied, "That's fine, Maggie, but before you go, let me make you a copy of our statement. It would be a good idea to reread it before we meet with Callahan."

Trip walked me out to my car, opened my door, and before I got in and drove away, he gave me a quick hug and a kiss saying, "I know we are doing the right thing, Maggie."

Chapter Thirty

W e were waiting for Callahan in Trip's office when the front desk receptionist called to announce his arrival; 9 a.m., right on time. Trip escorted Callahan back to his office, and they joined me at the conference table. Callahan cut through the chase, asking, "What is it you two know about these murders?"

Trip glanced at me, asking, "Do you want me to be the spokesperson for the two of us?"

I nodded in agreement.

Trip began by telling Callahan about the newspaper article he found in Hannah's personnel file, outlining their attempts to discover why it was in her file.

"Mentioned in the article was Albert Smith, who had been in a long-term relationship with Hannah since high school. We discovered that their relationship had recently ended. One of the other men mentioned in the article, Mark Singer, is currently employed as a bartender at the hotel and a friend of Albert."

Trip continued saying, "We also learned from Tim Swank, Superintendent of Schools, that Sara had turned down an invitation to the Prom. Rumor has it, this person still carries a grudge, but Swank had no idea who he was.

"Maggie and I spent a great deal of time viewing hotel entrance tapes from the security cameras for the periods surrounding the times of both Sara and Hannah's deaths. We were able to find the coming and goings of Sara, Albert, and Mark."

Trip told Callahan and me that he had checked Mark's timecard for the day of Hannah's murder before we arrived that morning. Mark was showing up on the back-door tape coming and going around the time of Hannah's murder, but he had only punched in and out during his night shift, 5 p.m. and 1:30 a.m. The question was, what was he doing in the hotel if he was not on the clock working?

On the morning of Hannah's death, Sara was on video entering the hotel. She had been attending a function in Meeting Room B but left the meeting during the 10:15 a.m. break putting her in direct proximity to the Board Room around the time of Hannah's murder.

Albert seemed to be in the clear he was in the bar the night Sara was murdered but had left the hotel minutes after Sara would have gone into the boardroom.

Finally, Trip told Callahan about Sara's estranged sister, Susan Milligan, checking into the hotel on Friday, the night before Sara's murder, and leaving Sunday, the day after her death. He stated that Susan was the person Sara had recently named in her will to inherit her estate. We have no idea if Susan contacted Sara or met with her while she was in town.

Trip through talking looked over at me and said, "Your turn."

I couldn't look at Callahan when I told him about driving to Albert's house. I didn't want to see the disapproving look he was sure to level on me!

I expressed my concern about Albert spotting me sitting in my car outside his dilapidated property and my fear that he might be trying to find out who I was. Looking up, sure enough, Callahan was looking quizzically at me.

"What on earth made you do that? That was a dangerous thing to do!"

"I freely admit it was not a brilliant idea, and I am sorry, but I felt Albert held the key to Hannah's and possibly Sara's murder. In my defense, Detective Callahan, it turned out to be helpful. Knowing what Albert looked like, I could spot him on the tapes. The irony is, we caught Albert on tape, but not during the time of either murder."

Before Callahan could respond, Trip continued, "Maggie and I are aware that several of these people had an opportunity to kill one or both women, and some with possible motives. We did not want to jeopardize your investigation by pursuing the murders any further."

Trip handed Callahan a box containing their statement, the tapes for the days of the murders, his hotel guest lists for both days, Mark's time cards, and a copy of the newspaper article about the missing money and credit card fraud.

Callahan rose to go and headed for the office door; before opening it, he looked back at us, saying, "I think I owe you both an explanation: The department thought Albert killed Hannah. He did not have an alibi for the day of her murder. That is why I didn't reach out to gather any more information. We were waiting for him to tip his hand in some way. We had no suspects for Sara's murder unless it was you two, a love triangle of sorts. Your perfect alibis left us 'clueless.'"

Then Callahan took a different stance saying, "I should chastise both of you for putting yourself in harm's way. If you had pursued the murders further, it could have tainted the evidence. I appreciate what you have both been going through and know your intentions were honorable.

I realize that you were trying to repair your impugned reputations and that of the hotel." He opened the door and left. Speechless and relieved, we exchanged a high five.

"So anticlimactic, I am not sure what to do with myself now."

Trip looked at his watch before saying, "Well, it is 10:45 a.m., and today is Wednesday; Rotary day. Are you going to be meeting with Tim Swank and his committee today?"

"No, the committee has completed its assignment."

"I should try to get some work done before the meeting, Maggie."

"I understand. I need to go home and freshen up before the luncheon." After the luncheon, I knew I would be overloaded, trying to read and critique the group project outlines and blueprints. Today would continue to be a very stressful day, with no chance to add relief with a walk.

Arriving home, with little time to spare, I quickly changed my clothes, checked my phone messages, and refreshed Lily's food and water dishes.

I walked into the Rotary Club luncheon pleased to find Trip had saved me a seat at a table he was sharing with three other people, none of whom I knew. I was hungry but aware that I was also feeding my emotional stress.

I didn't care if the food was gourmet or not today; I just needed it. Oh, my goodness, funny how you get what you need; comfort food. Today's lunch was meatloaf, au gratin potatoes, green beans, and a healthy slice of apple pie with vanilla ice cream. The meeting seemed to drag; I was anxious to get home and start writing my critiques of the student projects.

When I arrived home, I found Lily lying on the living room floor, basking in the sun shining through the front windows. I picked her up and gave her a quick cuddle and a kiss, gently placing her back in her sunny spot on the floor.

Entering my office, I sat down at my desk, resigned to settling in, for a long, tedious afternoon. I picked up an outline for the bridal event group. This group of female students, no surprise, were really into wedding planning. I wrote a page worth of notes providing them with friendly feedback about their plans.

Opening the next outline, I happened to look out my office window. My heart was racing when I saw a car parked across the street from my house; trying not to go into full panic mode, I grabbed my cell phone and dialed 911. Thank goodness employees respond quickly to those calls. I took a deep breath before saying, "Two men are sitting in a car parked in front of my house; one of them is Albert Smith, a person of interest in a murder investigation."

It seemed like forever, but I watched a police car pull up next to the parked car only minutes later. Two officers got out; one was Detective Barker. The officers approached the vehicle, flashed badges, and said something I couldn't hear. Albert and the other man got out of their car and raised their hands. The officers handcuffed them and helped both men slide into the back seat of the police cruiser. The officers got back into the police car and drove away.

By now, I was shaking like a leaf. I went into the living room, sat down on the sofa, and had a good cry. Lily, sensing something was wrong, settled herself in my lap. I couldn't help but wonder if they took the men to the police station for questioning. It certainly wasn't against the law to sit in front of someone's house; thank goodness, or they would have locked me up!

This encounter took all of fifteen minutes. It had only been a short time since Callahan had left the hotel; could he have already put out an APB (all-points bulletin) for those men? Knowing crime show vocabulary can come in handy.

Once I stopped crying and regained my composure, I called Trip, telling him about seeing Albert and a companion parked in front of my house. Before he could go into panic mode, I said, "Don't worry, I called 911, and Barker and another officer have already picked them up."

"That is a huge relief. With Albert off the streets, we won't have to worry about him harming you anymore."

"I am pretty sure Albert will be having a bad day, spending the better part of his afternoon in interrogation."

Trip chuckled, saying, "I hope so. I will call Callahan later today to find out what Albert had to say and get back to you with an update.

"I also need to remind Callahan that Albert breached the hotel security system. Perhaps Callahan will have some suggestions about making Albert pay the costs associated with restoring it."

Trip hung up, and I headed back to my office to continue working on feedback for blueprints and outlines. Teaching like everything else in life is a learning curve! Note to self; "Do not schedule two class projects for review at the same time ever again!"

Chapter Thirty-One

W hen Trip called me later that evening, he had quite a shocking story to tell! For starters, he updated me about his conversation with Angela, the hotel's front desk receptionist on duty at the time of Hannah's murder.

"Maggie, after meeting with us, Callahan wasted no time in interviewing Angela. Angela said she told Callahan she remembered talking to Sara that day. Sara had stopped at the front desk shortly after 10:30 a.m. asking for me. Angela told Sara that I was taking students on a hotel tour and was unsure when I would be free.

"Angela also told Callahan that Sara seemed distraught, and she asked Sara if she was alright. Sara had hesitated before saying something like, 'I will be fine once I get out of here and back to my shop.' However, Sara did not leave the hotel but instead headed in the direction of my office. The next time she saw Sara was shortly after 11 a.m. She was exiting through the front door of the hotel."

Trip continued his account, "I just got off the phone with Detective Callahan, another late night for him too. The man in the car with Albert was Mark, the bartender. Barker brought them both to the police station for questioning. Callahan and Barker interrogated them separately. Albert rolled on Mark.

"Not the brightest bulb, Albert admitted going to the hotel bar the night of Sara's murder and told Detective Callahan that Mark confessed to killing Hannah. Mark said she deserved it; she shouldn't have dumped Albert for someone else. When he learned Mark had murdered Hannah, the love of his life, Albert was furious. He didn't know what to do, so he left the hotel; he was only there for a short time."

Trip sighed, "It gets even more bizarre, Maggie. Albert told Callahan that Mark called him later that night, confiding that Sara was dead. Right-justifying his murdering her because Sara had seen him in the hallway outside the room where he had killed Hannah, leaving him no choice."

I interrupted Trip, saying, "Trip, it must have been Sara who covered Hannah with that tablecloth. Sara was wearing a very short mini skirt that day and was probably lying in a very undignified position. That was a thoughtful thing to do, but she should have come forward and told the police."

"Of course, it had to have been her, Maggie!"

I chimed in again, "If Albert was furious with Mark for killing Hannah, what was he doing sitting with him in a car outside my house?"

"After seeing Mark with Albert today, I am pretty sure it was Mark who dropped Albert off the day I was sitting in front of his house. Maybe I am judgmental, but at the very least, Albert should have reported both murders to the police as soon as he found out about them. Albert may not be totally off the hook."

Trip went on to say, "By the way, the night Hannah dumped Albert was the night Albert and Mark got arrested at that local bar and taken to the police station.

"As far as Susan goes, Maggie, Mark told Barker that Susan and Sara had both attended high school around the same time he did. Susan was two years older; she wasn't arrogant like her sister. She was part of their clique and had empathized with him when Sara had turned him down for the prom." Trip angrily, adding, "This guy is a wicked grudge holder; you had this right, Maggie.

"Callahan told me that Barker was able to get Mark to confess after he informed him that Albert had rolled on him. Mark told Barker that Susan had been drinking in the bar the Friday before Sara's death. After a few drinks, Susan confided that she had a copy of Sara's will. Her sister had named her the sole beneficiary of her estate. She wanted to find out what Sara's home and business might be worth. Susan said there was no love lost between the two of them. She and her sister and been estranged for years; Sara never wanted anything to do with her.

"According to Barker, grudge holder Mark admitted asking Susan how soon she would like to inherit that real estate? Susan told him she had been thinking about moving back to River Town. That is when they cooked up their plan to poison Sara.

"Mark told Barker that Susan called Sara late Saturday afternoon, and they agreed to meet at the bar at 5:45 p.m. Per their plan, she was to ask Sara to buy a bottle of wine for them to share, telling her she didn't have any money. Susan met Mark at the bar when he came on duty at 5 p.m. She handed him a pill bottle and whispered, 'This will do the trick.' He didn't know what it was and where she got it and didn't ask!"

"As expected, Sara arrived at the hotel bar at 5:45 p.m. She ordered a bottle of wine and two glasses telling him that her sister would be joining her. He opened the bottle and poured her a drink. Sara left her bar stool for a few minutes to talk to a couple she knew sitting at a table, providing him with an opportunity to lace her glass of wine. When she returned to the bar, he informed her that Susan had called and asked if there was a private place she and Sara could meet; he suggested the boardroom. Sara did as Susan asked, taking the bottle of wine, her glass, and one for Susan to the boardroom to meet up with her.

"Mark admitted Susan called him later that evening, telling him that she sat sipping a glass of wine while she and Sara talked about their childhood and the loss of their parents. When the poison finally took hold, Sara slumped forward over the table. After carefully removing her fingerprints from the bottle of wine and her glass, Susan told Mark that she had returned to her hotel room."

Trip finished his recount of Callahan's story, "Callahan called the local police in Clairton, Florida, asking them to pick up Susan. They were extraditing her to River Town; she and Mark Singer will be on trial for murder."

Maggie excitedly replied, "I can't believe, once we turned our information over to Callahan and Barker, they were able to wrap these murders up so quickly! We had the right people; we didn't know how the pieces fit together. I am sure Hannah's parents will be relieved that the police have arrested her murderer."

Trip cautioned, "I have a feeling this will hit the news tomorrow, so be prepared for more phone calls, maybe even from your boss."

Trip ended the call saying, "Maggie, I am exhausted and headed home. I will call you tomorrow."

"I am off to bed myself; sleep tight!"

Chapter Thirty-Two

My curiosity had the best of me, and tired as I was, I stumbled out of bed to watch the 6 a.m. local news. Putting on my bathrobe and slippers, I wandered into the kitchen to fix a cup of coffee before turning on the TV.

Trip was right. Making the news this morning was Officer Callahan. He was all smiles telling the reporter about the arrests of two suspects in connection with the murders of Hannah Johnson and Sara Milligan. He never mentioned the suspects' names or a warrant for the arrest of a third suspect.

Once again, Trip and I were in the news. However, there was nothing negative being reported about either of us by Callahan. He was singing our praises, telling the press that we had provided them with information leading to the arrests. He could have faulted us for overstepping our bounds or interfering with a police investigation, but he didn't—a savvy political move.

I had just finished breakfast when my phone rang. I figured it would be Dr. Caruthers, and it was. After our last "terse" conversation about the River Town Hotel and Conference

Center, I was a little warry about what she might have to say. It turned out; Dr. Caruthers was in a much better frame of mind today. I am sure that had something to do with the police arresting the killers, and I was not one of them.

She cautioned me not to make any statements to the press. As if I didn't already know that by now. I thanked her for the call and told her I would continue to abide by PSU's media policy.

I fully expected Susan Crenshaw to contact me and, of course, admonish me not to talk to the press.

I asked Dr. Caruthers if she would reconsider my class working with the hotel since the GM had no involvement in the murders —omitting that they had not stopped, but no harm, no foul from my point of view.

The silence before she responded was deafening, "I see no reason not to, as both of you are no longer considered suspects or involved in any way."

Why she thought I was a suspect was a mystery to me. I did not argue with her and thanked her, saying, "The students will be relieved."

I have been barraged with phone calls all morning. Concentrating on the student's blueprints and outlines with the phone ringing off the hook is next to impossible. I decided not to take any calls except from Trip or Susan Crenshaw; both checked in with me shortly after Dr. Carruthers.

Trip sounded better than he had the night before. I am sure the result of a good night's sleep and knowing our sleuthing days were behind us.

I told Trip about my conversation with Dr. Caruthers. He was pleased that she would let the group resume working on their hotel project, announcing, "Guess what? My calendar is open a week from this Friday at 10 a.m."

I laughed, telling him, "So is mine; we will be there."

I had been thinking about a way for Trip and me to cultivate our relationship. We could both use a little light-heartedness after all the murder drama. I planned on making a batch of homemade spaghetti and meatballs using my mom's special recipe on Saturday and asked him if he was free for dinner? He eagerly accepted. We hung up after that exchange.

We had both spent way too much time this week working on solving the murders and needed to play catch up with our job responsibilities!

Saturday night Trip arrived at 6 p.m. Over spaghetti and meatballs, a garden salad, and Italian bread, we talked about being bombarded with calls from newspapers and TV stations wanting to interview us. We were in demand because of our roles in catching the killers; naturally, we both declined.

Trip confided, "I am relieved that the phones are ringing non-stop with people wanting to book space at the hotel, now that it is safe and famous. The new director of sales and marketing is starting work on Monday, and I am hoping she will be able to take some of the pressure off."

I told him I understood and shared, "It was a huge relief to have finished my blueprints and outline reviews."

After dinner, we decided to watch a movie. We read the reviews touting the captivating murder mystery, *Handsome*—a Netflix Mystery Movie from 2017. "Satire's Homicide Detective Gene Handsome sets out to solve a woman's murder while searching for clues about what's missing from his personal life."

I winced, saying, "The plot is too close to the murder plots we just solved. How about we watch a rerun of *When Harry Met Sally?*"

"Good choice; I never tire of that movie."

We sat on the couch, snuggling, pausing for kisses in between, commenting on our favorite scenes as they unfolded. Lily was curled up next to us on the couch. Family TV night. It would be nice to have Trip's cats, Harry and Sally, here to join us! The evening ended all too early.

Chapter Thirty-Three

Wednesday, it is hard to believe a whole week has gone by since the police arrested the killers. I felt a little complacent—but grateful for the couch time with Lily and no anxiety attacks in the offing; over anything. It was a good thing Trip decided to call me early this morning to check in. I had forgotten about the Rotary Club Meeting today!

Tim Swank had suspended the Wednesday Fund-raising committee meetings. As the fundraising chair, all I need to do today is distribute raffle tickets to meeting attendees.

I had already eaten breakfast and quickly dressed in a navy-blue suit and a red, navy, and white floral print blouse. I spent the morning grading papers and headed over to the hotel fifteen minutes early with the intention of networking, of course!

Looking around the room, I saw Trip sitting at a table with his usual group of friends. He motioned for me to join them. I was delighted to be included. Once I was seated, the conversation resumed.

The 6 a.m. news and the arrest of Hannah's and Sara's killers was the hot topic at our table. Undoubtedly, some people will be dismayed when they learn the killers were locals and Trip's bartender was one of them. Poison and bartenders mentioned in the same breath or sentence don't work well! A marketing obstacle to overcome, if ever there was one.

Lunch was superb—chicken fettuccine alfredo, fresh-baked crescent rolls, butter, a beautifully presented peach cobbler with a scoop of vanilla ice cream for dessert. With full stomachs, the club members were ready to pay attention to the program.

The meeting highlight was Tim Swank's announcement, "Our fund-raiser will be a big money-maker if every member sells their allotted tickets. Maggie McManus will be distributing the cruise raffle tickets after the meeting today. Please stop by her table before you leave to sign for your allotment. Maggie, please stand up for a second so the members will know where to find you! A special thank you to my committee members for their commitment and hard work." As an afterthought, Tim added, "There is going to be a nice prize for the person selling the most tickets."

I am not sure where he came up with that; we never discussed it. But, if it motivates the members to sell tickets, so be it.

As my table mates rose from their seats, ready to go back to work, I handed each of them an envelope containing twenty raffle tickets and had them sign next to their names on a copy of the membership list.

A line formed at my table, and I continued handing out envelopes, having members sign for their tickets. This process took all of twenty minutes. Since President Wilson was still here, I gave him the membership list and the rest of the raffle ticket envelopes.

He thanked me, saying, "I will have my secretary mail them to the members who were not here today." As an after-thought, adding, "Maggie, I will see that the Club Treasurer gets the money and any unsold tickets."

I was relieved to be off the hook! "Thank you, President Wilson; I am happy to hear that and hope the sales go well." I was now free to head home and resume working on my courses.

Friday morning, I drove over to the hotel for my 10 a.m. meeting with Trip and the students. We learned that the new Sales and Marketing Director, Cynthia Stephens, would not be involved in the group project; Trip would continue working with us. "Cynthia," he said, "needs to focus on getting acclimated to all the other aspects of her new job."

With the blueprints completed, the next phase was to interview guests about their experiences with the hotel staff. Guest interaction is where the fun begins for the students. Trip set up times, dates, and meeting rooms for the group to meet with registered guests over the next few weeks. I gave Trip a copy of the questionnaire the class had developed and would be using to conduct the interviews. The meeting was productive, and time passed quickly. The students left the boardroom, and I rose to follow them out. Trip stopped me asking, "Can you stay for a few minutes? I have something to talk to you about?"

Trip excitedly said, "I reserved a date with the catering staff for my housewarming. I am sorry I didn't confirm the time with you first, but there were only a few dates left in November because of Thanksgiving and holiday parties. I didn't want to miss out and settled on the second Saturday in November from 6 p.m. until 10 p.m."

I smiled, saying, "Not to worry, I am available. I have a limited social life that seems to revolve primarily around you."

Trip laughed, "I am delighted to hear that. Does that mean you are free to come over to my house Sunday afternoon to help plan the party? I will bring the catering menus home with me today, so I don't forget them. I would appreciate your help selecting the menu and thinking about how best to arrange the house for this gathering. I will start the guest list, and we can look it over together. There may be people you think I have overlooked or friends you may want to invite."

After thanking him for his thoughtfulness, I headed home.

I arrived at Trip's house Sunday at 2 p.m. Trip ushered me into the kitchen, saying, "The guest list is close to being completed. Before I forget to tell you, I called my parents, and they seemed delighted to be coming to stay with me and are looking forward to the housewarming party. I suggested they arrive Friday at noon to have some alone time before the party on Saturday. They seem eager to patch things up between us."

"I am so happy for you, Trip; your reunion with your parents is long overdue."

We sat down at the kitchen table, and Trip handed me the first page of his two-page list, complete with addresses. By the time I finished reading it, Trip had completed the second page. I picked it up and, after studying the names, said, "Trip, you might want to consider the Rotary Club President, Robert Wilson, and his wife, Betty."

"Good catch, Maggie. I would have felt awful if I missed them, and that would be akin to business suicide." He added their names to the guest list.

The guest list now totaled thirty people, including Trip and me. We realized not all thirty people would attend, but at least we invited them.

Next, we walked from room to room, looking for a place to set up a bar. We agreed that Trip should hire a bartender, even though he would offer a limited selection of wines, beer, and basic cocktails. We finally decided on a corner in the family room, the room furthest away from the dining room where the catering staff would be serving the food.

The menu was our next challenge. If all thirty people show up, seating will be a concern; people may need to stand while eating their food. We agreed to keep the menu simple.

Trip suggested having the caterers set up a buffet line in the dining room. The catering staff would set out the food around 7:15 p.m. We decided on an Italian theme; a garden salad, oil and vinegar dressing, Italian bread, and two entrees—asparagus and shrimp with angel hair pasta and chicken fettuccine alfredo.

In keeping with our Italian theme, we chose an antipasto platter of cured meats, olives, pepperoncini, mushrooms, anchovies, artichokes hearts, various cheeses, pickled meats, and vegetables in oil and vinegar. The catering staff would pass the platters as appetizers shortly after 6 p.m. Passing the appetizers would allow guests to chat with each other and prevent a bottleneck at an hor d'ourves' station.

Trip decided it would be easiest to have the local bakery make a sheet cake for dessert. We could serve coffee and cake in the kitchen after the caterers departed, freeing up the kitchen space. We estimated the catering staff would be wrapping up around 9:00 p.m. and, if warranted, the bar would remain open until the party ended at 10 p.m.

That done, Trip reached over and enveloped me in a big bear hug. "I am relieved we have the planning out of the way, and I can meet with the catering manager tomorrow to discuss our plans."

"Trip, can you get invitations printed in time; the party is two weeks away?"

"I am pretty sure I can. I have used a printer that has done jobs for the hotel in a day. Hopefully, they can provide a one-day turnaround! I want to get them addressed and mailed mid-week."

I offered to help, but Trip said, "I can handle it. I will include an RSVP to my office phone number so I can provide the caterers with an accurate headcount."

The following week was routine, except for dinner Saturday evening at the Texas Roadhouse. Nothing fancy, but their steaks are always excellent. After dinner, we drove to the river, parked the car, and walked hand in hand along the River Walk, admiring the local's boats moored in their slips. Talking about ordinary everyday things, food, friends, work, aspirations for the future, and the upcoming housewarming party was refreshing.

Chapter Thirty-Four

T he following Friday, Trip's parents arrived. He called me that evening after his parents had gone to bed. I knew this was a big day for him, and he needed someone to listen. I was delighted he had chosen me!

"Maggie, I had a good beginning with my parents today. Mom and Dad arrived at the hotel at noon as planned, and I took them on a hotel tour before lunch. I walked them through the ballroom, the kitchen, and the boardroom; they seemed agile enough. Their questions indicated I did not need to worry about their loss of mental acuity, which was a huge relief. After the tour, we had lunch in the dining room. Mom and Dad were pleased to find our all-time family favorite, fish and chips, on the menu."

I knew Trip wasn't finished and waited for him to continue. "My parents followed me home from, the hotel. I could tell they were impressed as they entered the house. Unfortunately, the guest rooms are all on the second floor, but having gauged their mobility, I wasn't concerned. I deposited their suitcases in the largest guest room, and when I came back down, I found Mom wandering around the house. She told me she loved my home. 'It was perfect for a family.'

"Dad found the television remote and was content to settle on the couch, searching for a news channel. As it turned out, we spent the afternoon reminiscing about my childhood. Harry and Sally finally surfaced, and they settled on the couch next to Dad. Mom and Dad didn't want to go out to dinner; they were both tired from a long day of traveling. I ordered pizza delivery, and my parents went to bed at 8 p.m."

Trip hesitated for a moment before continuing, and I knew we had reached the moment in his account that listening to him was paramount! Something was bothering him, and he had difficulty deciding how to express his concerns.

He finally said," I know my parents have just arrived, and it was a long trip, but I am concerned about them. My parents have always been energetic, enthusiastic, and full of life; I felt positive around them until Sissy divorced me. Something is amiss, and it is not just about them being older. They don't seem very upbeat. Even asking them about their travel plans didn't spark them.

"Tomorrow I have to go to work, but Mom and Dad told me that was fine, they wanted to check out the area for themselves, and Mom wants to do some shopping."

"Be patient with them, Trip. You will have time over the weekend to address your concerns and find out what's wrong. I am looking forward to the housewarming party tomorrow and the chance to meet your parents. I will be over at 5:00 p.m. to help tie up loose ends."

When I arrived at Trip's house, the caterers were just starting to set up, and I placed the floral centerpiece I brought with me on the dining room table. Trip and I worked with the caterers setting up the buffet table and finding places to put the food and supplies they had brought. The bartender arrived at 5:30 p.m. and began setting up the bar in the family room.

Trip's parents came downstairs shortly after the bartender arrived. Trip brought them into the kitchen to meet me, possessively putting his arm around my waist, saying, "Mom and Dad, I want you to meet my girlfriend, Maggie McManus. Maggie is a former GM and is now a college professor at Panhandle State University. Maggie, meet my mother, Mary, and my father, Clarence."

Mary and Clarence were cordial but reserved, not quite the reception I anticipated. There were no hugs, handshakes, or an acknowledgment of me being Trip's girlfriend. I told them I was delighted to meet them and hoped they would enjoy themselves.

His parents stiffly excused themselves and went to the bar to order a drink. They settled down on the couch in the family room.

Guests started arriving at 6 p.m. sharp. Trip spent time standing at the door greeting people, and I ushered them into the family room, pointing them toward the bar. The caterers were in full swing by 6:15 p.m., passing the antipasto appetizer trays. Most of the guests had arrived by then, and people were standing in groups animatedly talking and laughing. Trip and I separated, walking between the rooms joining in on conversations. People seem to be having a good time eating and keeping the bartender busy.

At 6:45 p.m., the doorbell rang. Trip answered the door; I looked over, fully expecting it to be guests who were running late; but there on the steps stood a woman I did not know, holding the hand of a little girl. Trip looked on in horror as his father grabbed the woman's arm, bringing the woman and child into his home.

I quickly put two and two together and realized it was Sissy and her daughter Abigail. Trip's father must have expected her; why else would he be waiting by the door for Trip to open it? Trip's mother joined them in the hallway, obviously a party to this deception. Abigail threw herself into her arms, and his mother was hugging and kissing her. When did she become so close to Sissy's daughter?

Trip seemed to be in a state of shock, not knowing what to do. His mother took Abigail and Sissy into the family room, and they sat together on the sofa while Trip's father approached the bar ordering a glass of wine for Sissy and another scotch on the rocks for himself.

Sissy left Abigail on the couch with Trip's mother, and she and his father started mingling with the guests. I was sure Trip had no idea his parents planned for Sissy to crash his party. I am also sure he was concerned about who Sissy was telling his guests she was! I knew it wasn't going to be good. I think we just found out why his parents had been acting subdued; they had planned all along to disrupt Trip's housewarming party.

I watched Sissy working the room, wangling her way into conversations. Sissy was outgoing; her slim appearance, expressive green eyes, perfect skin, and straight, pale blond hair extending halfway down her back were turning heads. I noticed that she had pulled her hair back with an intricate jade hair clip, a perfect accessory for her form-fitting, ankle-length dress reminiscent of a Japanese Kimono. Jade stud earrings completed her ensemble. The embossed, pale green dress perfectly matched her eyes, and she knew it!

Out of the corner of my eye, I saw her heading my way. Trip caught that too, but I waved him away, and he joined another group of people. Sissy did not acknowledge knowing I was Trip's girlfriend. Instead, she introduced herself as Trip's ex-wife, saying they hoped to get back together. I knew that was not true, or at least I hoped it wasn't. But then why was she here? What made her think she could walk back into Trip's life? I responded, "Good luck to both of you," and excused myself to join Clara and Ralph.

The dinner service went without a hitch. Standing alongside Clara and Ralph, I ate dinner, keeping one eye on Sissy, who had settled on the couch, eating dinner companionably with Trip's parents. After dinner, I watched Trip's mother take Abigail upstairs. Sissy remained seated with Trip's father in the family room. They seemed so pleased with themselves. How could they not know the damage they had done! I did my best to get through the evening; I wandered around in a fog, trying to mingle and be sociable.

Finally, at last, the caterers packed up and departed, and it was time for coffee and dessert. I went into the kitchen and found Jennifer and Clara already cutting the cake and pouring coffee. I couldn't wait for this evening to be over.

Jennifer reached out gave me a huge hug, saying, "I am so sorry this happened, but I am proud of you and Trip for being such troopers and not causing a ruckus in front of the guests."

Trip showed up at my side, apologizing profusely; thoroughly agitated by this unbelievable situation! I felt so sorry for him, reaching up, gently kissing him on the cheek; I whispered in his ear, "This too shall pass; stay strong."

The last of the guests left at 10:15 p.m. I was right behind them, saying, "I know you have a lot to deal with, Trip. Please call me after you get sorted out, and you are free to talk."

Trip hugged me, telling me he would call as soon as he could. He let go of me, and I walked toward the front door. I felt no compunction about not saying goodbye to Trip's parents. I could hear Jennifer saying, "Call me tomorrow, Trip. I will be on pins and needles until I hear the outcome of your family trauma."

When I arrived home, I was so pent up I knew I wouldn't be able to sleep. I sat reliving the evening with sweet Lily in my lap. Were his parents intentionally cruel or perhaps just clueless about what they had done to Trip by bringing Sissy and Abigail to his house warming party?

I watched his mother, Mary, interact with Abigail. Mary adored that little girl and had become a grandmother to her. It was apparent when her second marriage failed, and Trip moved away from home that, in time, Sissy had inserted herself into Trip's parent's life. Trip shutting his parents out and losing contact with them for so many years played into her hand, and Sissy and Abigail became the center of his parent's world.

I sat wondering about what was going on at Trip's house. I had no idea what Trip would do after the last guest left! He hated conflict and could easily become a pawn in his parent's plan to reunite him with Sissy. There is nothing I can do about it; his parents had treated me with indifference and obviously thought I was in the way of Trip reuniting with Sissy. All I can do is wait for Trip to call and hope he had enough nerve to stand up to all of them. I wasn't sure how I would react if the outcome were unfavorable. I am still grieving my mother, and Trip has become my world. His parent's deception had him flustered, but after the events of this evening, I wasn't feeling so emotionally secure myself.

Confucius —*Wisdom, compassion, and courage are the three universally recognized moral qualities of men.* I will need to embrace these qualities to help me get through this.